Too Loud a Solitude

Other books by Bohumil Hrabal

I SERVED THE KING OF ENGLAND
CLOSELY WATCHED TRAINS
THE LITTLE TOWN WHERE TIME STOOD STILL

BOHUMIL HRABAL

Too Loud a Solitude

Translated from the Czech by
MICHAEL HENRY HEIM

A Harvest Book · Harcourt, Inc.
San Diego   New York   London

For information about permission to reproduce
selections from this book, write to Permissions,
Houghton Mifflin Harcourt Publishing Company,
215 Park Avenue South, New York, New York 10003.

This translation of *Too Loud a Solitude* appeared, in slightly
different form, in *Cross Currents: A Yearbook of Central European
Culture*, Volume 5, Ann Arbor, 1986.

Library of Congress Cataloging-in-Publication Data
Hrabal, Bohumil, 1914–
[Příliš hlučná samota. English]
Too loud a solitude/Bohumil Hrabal; translated from
the Czech by Michael Henry Heim.—1st U.S. ed.
p. cm.
Translation of: Příliš hlučná samota.
ISBN 0-15-190491-X
ISBN 0-15-690458-6 (pbk.)
ISBN 978-0-15-690458-2 (pbk)
I. Title.
PG5039.18.R2P713   1990   90-4313
891.8′635—dc20

Designed by Camilla Filancia
Printed in the United States of America
DOC 30 29 28 27 26 25 24 23 22 21

Only the sun has a right to its spots.

—GOETHE

Too Loud a Solitude

O N E

For thirty-five years now I've been in wastepaper, and it's my love story. For thirty-five years I've been compacting wastepaper and books, smearing myself with letters until I've come to look like my encyclopedias—and a good three tons of them I've compacted over the years. I am a jug filled with water both magic and plain; I have only to lean over and a stream of beautiful thoughts flows out of me. My education has been so unwitting I can't quite tell which of my thoughts come from me and which from my books, but that's how I've stayed attuned to myself and the world around me for the past thirty-five years. Because when I read, I don't really read; I pop a beautiful sentence into my mouth and suck it like a fruit drop, or I sip it like a liqueur until the thought dissolves in me like alcohol, infusing brain and heart and coursing on through the veins to the root of each blood vessel. In an average month I compact two tons of books, but to muster the strength for my godly labors I've drunk so much beer over the past thirty-five years that it could fill an Olympic pool, an entire fish hatchery. Such wisdom as I have has come to me unwittingly, and I look on my brain as a mass of hydraulically compacted thoughts, a bale of ideas, and my head as a smooth, shiny Aladdin's lamp. How much more beautiful it must have been in the days when the only place a thought could make its mark was the human brain and anybody wanting to squelch ideas had to compact human heads, but even that wouldn't have helped, because real thoughts come from outside and travel with us like the noodle soup we take to work; in other words, inquisitors burn books in vain. If a book has anything to say, it burns with a quiet laugh, because any book worth its salt points up and out of itself. I've just bought one of those minuscule adder-subtractor-square-rooters, a tiny little contraption no bigger than a wallet, and after screwing up my courage I pried open the back with a screwdriver, and was I shocked and tickled to find nothing but an even tinier contraption—smaller than a postage stamp and thinner than ten pages of a book—that and air, air charged with mathematical variations. When my eye lands on a real book and looks past the printed word, what it sees is disembodied thoughts flying through air, gliding on air, living off air, returning to air, because in the end everything is air, just as the host is and is not the blood of Christ.

For thirty-five years now I've been compacting old

paper and books, living as I do in a land that has known how to read and write for fifteen generations; living in a onetime kingdom where it was and still is a custom, an obsession, to compact thoughts and images patiently in the heads of the population, thereby bringing them ineffable joy and even greater woe; living among people who will lay down their lives for a bale of compacted thoughts. And now it is all recurring in me. Along with thirty-five years of pushing the red and green buttons on my hydraulic press, I've had thirty-five years of drinking beer—not that I enjoy it, no, I loathe drunkards, I drink to make me think better, to go to the heart of what I read, because what I read I read not for the fun of it or to kill time or fall asleep; I, who live in a land that has known how to read and write for fifteen generations, drink so that what I read will prevent me from falling into everlasting sleep, will give me the d.t.'s, because I share with Hegel the view that a noble-hearted man is not yet a nobleman, nor a criminal a murderer. If I knew how to write, I'd write a book about the greatest of man's joys and sorrows. It is by and from books that I've learned that the heavens are not humane, neither the heavens nor any man with a head on his shoulders— it's not that men don't wish to be humane, it just goes against common sense. Rare books perish in my press, under my hands, yet I am unable to stop their flow: I am nothing but a refined butcher. Books have taught me the joy of devastation: I love cloudbursts and demolition crews, I can stand for hours watching the carefully co-ordinated pumping motions of detonation experts as they blast entire houses, entire streets, into the air while seeming only to fill tires. I can't get enough of that first moment, the one that lifts all the bricks and stones and beams only to cave them in quietly, like clothes dropping, like a steamer sinking swiftly to the ocean floor when its boilers have burst. There I stand in the cloud of dust, in the music of fulmination, thinking of my work deep down in the cellar where I have my press, the one where I've been working for thirty-five years by the light of a few electric bulbs and where above me I hear steps moving across the courtyard, and, through an opening in the ceiling, which is also a hole in the middle of the courtyard, I see heaven-sent horns of plenty in the form of bags, crates, and boxes raining down their old paper, withered flower-shop stalks, wholesalers' wrappings, out-of-date theater programs, ice-cream wrappers, sheets of paint-spattered wallpaper, piles of moist, bloody paper from the butchers', razor-sharp rejects from photographers' studios, insides of office wastepaper baskets, typewriter ribbons included, bouquets from birthdays and namedays long past. Sometimes I find a cobblestone buried in a bundle of newspapers to make it weigh more or a penknife and a pair of scissors disposed of by mistake, or claw hammers or cleavers or cups with dried black coffee still in them, or faded wedding nosegays wound round with fresh artificial funeral wreaths.

For thirty-five years I've been compacting it all in my hydraulic press, and three times a week it is transported by truck to train and then on to the paper mill, where they snap the wires and dump my work into alkalis and acids strong enough to dissolve the razor blades I keep gouging my hands with. But just as a beautiful fish will occasionally sparkle in the waters of a polluted river that runs through a stretch of factories, so in the flow of old paper the spine of a rare book will occasionally shine forth, and if for a moment I turn away, dazzled, I always turn back in time to rescue it, and after wiping it off on my apron, opening it wide, and breathing in its print, I glue my eyes to the text and read out the first sentence like a Homeric prophecy; then I place it carefully among my other splendid finds in a small crate lined with the holy cards someone once dropped into my cellar by mistake with a load of prayer books, and then comes my ritual, my mass: not only do I read every one of those books, I take each and put it in a bale, because I have a need to garnish my bales, give them my stamp, my signature, and I always worry about whether I've made a bale distinctive enough: I have to spend two hours overtime in the cellar every working day, I have to get to work an hour early, I sometimes have to come in on Saturdays if I want to work my way through the never-ending mountain of old paper. Last month they delivered nearly fifteen hundred pounds of "Old Masters" reproductions, dropped nearly fifteen hundred pounds of sopping-wet Rembrandts, Halses, Monets, Manets, Klimts, Cézannes, and other big guns of European art into my cellar, so now I frame each of my bales with reproductions, and when evening comes and the bales stand one next to the other waiting in all their splendor for the service elevator, I can't take my eyes off them: now *The Night Watch*, now *Saskia*, here *Le Déjeuner sur l'herbe*, there the *House of the Hanged Man at Anvers* or *Guernica*. Besides, I'm the only one on earth who knows that deep in the heart of each bale there's a wide-open *Faust* or *Don Carlos*, that here, buried beneath a mound of blood-soaked cardboard, lies a *Hyperion*, there, cushioned on piles of cement bags rests a *Thus Spake Zarathustra*; I'm the only one on earth who knows which bale has Goethe, which Schiller, which Hölderlin, which Nietzsche. In a sense, I am both artist and audience, but the daily pressure does me in, tires me out, racks me, sears me, and to reduce and restrict my enormous self-output I drink beer after beer, and on my way to Husenský's for refills I have time to meditate and dream about what my next bale is going to look like. The only reason I down so much beer is to see into the future, because in every bale I bury a precious relic, a child's open coffin strewn with withered flowers, tinsel, and angel's hair, and I make a nice little bed for the books that turn up unexpectedly in the cellar, much as I myself turned up there one day. That's why I'm always behind in my work, why the courtyard is piled to the rooftops with old paper that can't go down the opening in the ceiling of my cellar for the mountain of old paper blocking it from below; that's why my boss, his face scarlet with rage, will sometimes stick his hook through the opening and clear away enough paper to shout down to me, "Haňťa! Where are you? For Christ's sake, will you stop ogling those books and get to work? The courtyard's piled high with paper and you sit there dreaming!" And I huddle in the lee of my paper mountain like Adam in the bushes and pick up a book, and my eyes open panic-stricken on a world other than my own, because when I start reading I'm somewhere completely different, I'm in the text, it's amazing, I have to admit I've been dreaming, dreaming in a land of great beauty, I've been in the very heart of truth. Ten times a day, every day, I wonder at having wandered so far, and then, alienated from myself, a stranger to myself, I go home, walking the streets silently and in deep meditation, passing trams and cars and pedestrians in a cloud of books, the books I found that day and am carrying home in my briefcase. Lost in my dreams, I somehow cross at the traffic signals, never bumping into street lamps or people, yet moving onward, exuding fumes of beer and grime, yet smiling, because my briefcase is full of books and that very night I expect them to tell me things about myself I don't know. On I go through the noisy streets, never crossing at the red; I walk subconsciously unconscious, half-asleep, subliminally inspired, with every bale I've compacted that day fading softly and quietly inside me. I have a physical sense of myself as a bale of compacted books, the seat of a tiny pilot light of karma, like the flame in a gas refrigerator, an eternal flame I feed daily with the oil of my thoughts, which come from what I unwittingly read during work in the books I am now taking home in my briefcase. So I walk home like a burning house, like a burning stable, the light of life pouring out of the fire, fire pouring out of the dying wood, hostile sorrow lingering under the ashes.

For thirty-five years now I've been compacting old paper in my hydraulic press. I've got five years till retirement and my press is going with me, I won't abandon it, I'm saving up, I've got my own bankbook and the press and me, we'll retire together, because I'm going to buy it from the firm, I'm going to take it home and stash it somewhere among the trees in my uncle's garden, and then, when the time is right, I'll make only one bale a day, but what a bale, a bale to end all bales, a statue, an artifact, I'll pour all my youthful illusions into it, everything I know, everything I've learned during my thirty-five years of work; at last I'll work only when the spirit moves me, when I feel inspired, one bale a day from the three tons of books I have waiting at home, a bale I'll never need to be ashamed of, a bale I'll have time to think out, dream out, in advance. And, more important, while I line the drum of my press with books and old paper, while I'm in the throes of creation but just before I turn the pressure on, I'll sprinkle it all with confetti and sequins, a new bale a day, and when a year is up—an exhibition, I'll hold a bale exhibition in the garden, and all the people who come will be able to make their own, though under my supervision, and when the green light goes on and the press starts churning, starts its tremendously powerful churning, starts crushing and compacting the old paper trimmed with books and flowers and whatever refuse people happen to have brought along, the sensitive spectator will personally experience compaction in my hydraulic press.

But now I'm at home, sitting on a chair, my head drooping lower and lower, until I drift off the only way I know how, moist lips against raised knees. Sometimes I remain in my Thonet position as late as midnight, and when I awake, curled up, coiled up in myself like a cat in winter, like a rocking-chair frame, I lift my head to find my trouser knee drenched with drool. I can be by myself because I'm never lonely, I'm simply alone, living in my heavily populated solitude, a harum-scarum of infinity and eternity, and Infinity and Eternity seem to take a liking to the likes of me.

T W O

For thirty-five years now I've been compacting old paper, and I've had so many beautiful books tossed into my cellar that if I had three barns they'd all be full. Just after the war was over—the second one—somebody dumped a basket of the most exquisitely made volumes in my hydraulic press, and when I'd calmed down enough to open one of them, what did I see but the stamp of the Royal Prussian Library, and when next day I found the whole cellar overflowing with more of the same— leather-bound tomes, their gilt edges and titles flooding the air with light—I raced upstairs to see two fellows standing there, and what I managed to squeeze out of them was that somewhere in the vicinity of Nové Strašecí there was a barn with so many books in the straw it made your eyes pop out of your head. So I went to see the army librarian, and the two of us took off for Nové

Straseci, and there in the fields we found not one but three barns chock full of the Royal Prussian Library, and once we'd done oohing and ahing, we had a good talk, as a result of which a column of military vehicles spent a week transporting the books to a wing of the Ministry of Foreign Affairs in Prague, where they were to wait until things simmered down, when they could be sent back to their place of origin. But somebody leaked the hiding place and the Royal Prussian Library was declared official booty, so the column of military vehicles started transporting all the leather-bound tomes with their gilt edges and titles over to the railroad station, where they were loaded on flatcars in the rain, and since it poured the whole week, what I saw when the last load of books pulled up was a constant flow of gold water and soot and printer's ink coming from the train. Well, I just stood there, leaning against a lamppost, flabbergasted, and as the last car disappeared into the mist, I felt the rain on my face merging with tears, so when on my way out of the station I saw a policeman in uniform, I crossed my wrists and begged him with the utmost sincerity to take out his handcuffs, his bracelets, as we used to call them, and take me in—I'd committed a crime, a crime against humanity—and when he did take me in, all they did was laugh at me and threaten to lock me up. A few more years of the same, though, and I got used to it: I would load entire libraries from country castles and city mansions, fine, rare, leather- and Morocco-bound books, load whole trains full, and as soon as a train had thirty cars, off it would go to Switzerland or Austria, one kilogram of rare books for the equivalent of one crown in convertible currency, and nobody blinked an eye, nobody shed a tear, not even I myself, no, all I did was stand there smiling as I watched the train hauling those priceless libraries off to Switzerland and Austria for one crown in convertible currency a kilo. By then I had mustered the strength to look upon misfortune with composure, to still my emotions, by then I had begun to understand the beauty of destruction, and I loaded more and more freight cars, and more and more trains left the station heading west at one crown per kilogram, and as I stood there staring after the red lantern hanging from the last car, as I stood there leaning on a lamppost like Leonardo da Vinci, who stood leaning on a column and looking on while French soldiers used his statue for target practice, shooting away horse and rider bit by bit, I thought how Leonardo, like me, standing and witnessing such horrors with complete composure, had realized even then that neither the heavens are humane nor is any man with a head on his shoulders.

At about that time I received word that my mother was dying, so I immediately hopped on my bike and rode home, but since I happened to be thirsty, I ran down to the cellar and grabbed a cold earthenware jug of sour milk, picked it up with both hands, and was gulping it down greedily when all at once I saw two eyes floating opposite my own, but I was so thirsty that I went on drinking until the two eyes were as dangerously close as the lights of a locomotive speeding into a tunnel at night, and suddenly the eyes disappeared and my mouth was full of something wrigglingly alive, and I pulled a frog out of it by the leg, and as soon as I had disposed of it in the garden, I went back and polished off the milk à la Leonardo. When Mama died, I cried a bit to myself, but never shed a tear. Leaving the crematorium, I watched the smoke rising from the chimney into the sky, watched Mama making her way upward to the heavens, but before leaving I decided to take a trip downstairs: after all, didn't they do in their cellar with people what I did in my cellar with books? Anyway, I waited until the service was over and watched them burning four corpses, the third of which was Mama, looked on motionless at the final state of man, observed my counterpart picking out the bones, grinding them in his hand mill, grinding up Mama, too, and laying her earthly remains in a metal box, and all I could do was stand there and stare—the way I stared after the train taking those wonderful libraries off to Switzerland and Austria at one convertible crown a kilo—stand there and think of the lines from Sandburg about how all that remains of a man is the phosphorus for a box of matches or the iron for a noose-worthy nail.

A month later I got them to sign the urn over to me, and when I took Mama's ashes to my uncle, carried them out to his garden and up to his signal tower, he called out to them, "Home again at last, eh, Sis?" And when I gave him the urn, he weighed it in his hand and declared she wasn't quite all there—she'd weighed a full one hundred and sixty-five pounds when she was alive—so he weighed her on a scale and then sat down and worked out that there ought to be another one and three-quarter ounces of her. Anyway, he placed the urn on a wardrobe, and once that summer, while he was hoeing out the kohlrabi, he thought of his sister, my mother, and how she loved kohlrabi, so he took down the urn and opened it with a bottle opener and scattered Mama's ashes over the kohlrabi, which we later ate. For a long time thereafter I would hear the crunch of human skeletons whenever my hydraulic press entered its final phase and crushed the beautiful books with a force of twenty atmospheres, I would hear the crunch of human skeletons and feel I was grinding up the skulls and bones of press-crushed classics, the part of the Talmud that says: "For we are like olives: only when we are crushed do we yield what is best in us."

After the crushing is over, I do up each bale with steel bands, pulling them as tight as possible, so that, try as the books may to break out, the steel holds, and I think of the full-to-bursting chest of the sideshow strongman who rends his chains by forcing yet more air into his lungs. But the bale is safe in the strong embrace of the steel bands, everything is as calm inside as inside the burial urn, and I reverently dolly it over to its mates, making sure to turn it so that the reproductions face me. Because this week I've started in on a hundred reproductions of Rembrandt van Rijn, a hundred portraits of the old artist with the mushroom face, the face of a man pushed to the brink of eternity by art and drink, the door handle starting to turn, the final door pushed open from without by an unknown hand, and I'm beginning to have his puff-paste face, that peeling, piss-soaked wall of a face, I'm beginning to smile his half-moronic smile, to look at the world from the other side of human causes and events, and all my bales these days are framed with that portrait of Rembrandt van Rijn as an old man while I keep filling my drum with wastepaper and open books.

Today for the first time I noticed I'd stopped looking out for the mice, their nests, their families. When I throw in blind baby mice, the mother jumps in after them, sticks by them, and shares the fate of my classics and wastepaper. You wouldn't believe how many mice there are in a cellar like mine, two hundred, five hundred maybe, most of them friendly little creatures born half-blind, but there's one thing we have in common, namely, a vital need for literature with a marked preference for Goethe and Schiller in Morocco bindings. My cellar is constantly full of blinkings and gnawings: in their free time the mice are as playful as kittens, climbing up and down the sides of the press and pattering along the horizontal shaft. Then the green button sets the drum wall in motion and throws paper and mice into a high-stress situation, and the cheeping fades and the mice in other parts of the cellar suddenly turn serious and stand on their hind legs, prick up their ears, wondering what those new noises are, but since mice lose track of the moment as soon as the moment is over, they go right back to their games, to munching books, the older the paper the tastier it is, like a well-aged cheese or vintage wine. My life is so tightly bound up with these mice that even though I give all the paper a good evening hosing, which for the mice is like a daily dunking, they're always in a good mood and even look forward to their bath: they enjoy the aftermath, hours of licking and warming themselves in their paper retreats. Sometimes I lose control over my mice: I go out for a beer, lost in deep meditation, I dream as I wait at the bar, and when I open my coat to reach for my wallet, out jumps a mouse on the counter, or when I leave, out scurries a pair from a trouser leg, and the waitresses go wild, climb on chairs, stick their fingers in their ears, and scream bloody murder. And I just smile and wave a wet good-bye, full of plans for my next bale.

For thirty-five years now I've been throwing each bale into a high-stress situation, crossing off every year, every month, every day in the month until we both retire, my press and I. I've been bringing home books every evening in my briefcase, and my two-floor Holešovice apartment is all books: what with the cellar and the shed long since packed and the kitchen, pantry, and even bathroom full, the only space free is a path to the window and stove. Even the bathroom has only room enough for me to sit down in: just above the toilet bowl, about five feet off the floor, I have a whole series of shelves, planks piled high to the ceiling, holding over a thousand pounds of books, and one careless roost, one careless rise, one brush with a shelf, and half a ton of books would come tumbling down on me, catching me with my pants down. And when there was no room for even a single addition, I pushed my twin beds together and rigged a kind of canopy of planks over them, ceiling high, for the two additional tons of books I've carried home over the years, and when I fall asleep I've got all those books weighing down on me like a two-ton nightmare. Sometimes, when I'm careless enough to turn in my sleep or call out or twitch, I am horrified to hear the books start to slide, because it would take little more than a raised knee or a shout to bring them all down like an avalanche, a cornucopia of rare books, and squash me like a flea. There are nights when I think that the books are plotting against me for compacting a hundred innocent mice a day, that they want to get even with me, and well they might: our transgressions haunt us. I lie on my back half drunk under a canopy of miles and miles of texts, trying hard not to remember, but then I'll think of the time the local forester caught a marten in an inside-out sleeve lining and, instead of killing it, justly, for having gobbled up some chickens, he took a nail, hammered it into its head, and then let it go darting and howling around the yard until it died. And then I'll remember how a year later the forester's son was killed by a live wire while repairing a cement mixer. Just yesterday the figure of the forester came back to me, out of the blue, under my canopy, and I remembered him sharpening a stick each time he came across a hedgehog curled up in a ball and sinking that sharp stick into the hedgehog's stomach— he was too cheap to waste a bullet—until one day he took to bed with cancer of the liver and in return for all those hedgehogs he spent three long months curled up in a ball, a tumor in his stomach and horror in his brain, before he died. Such are the thoughts that make me panic when I hear the books above me plotting their revenge, and I am so terrified by the prospect of having them flatten me and then crash through each floor all the way to the basement, like an elevator, that I prefer sleeping in my chair by the window. The way I look at it, my life fits together beautifully: at work I have books—and bottles and inkwells and staplers—raining down on me through the opening in the cellar ceiling, and at home I have books above me constantly threatening to fall and kill or at least maim me. The swords of Damocles that I've hung from my bathroom and bedroom ceilings force me to make as many trips for beer at home as at work: it's my only defense against a beautiful misery.

Once a month I go and visit my uncle and look around in his garden for the place to put my press when we retire. The idea of saving up and buying the hydraulic press when I retire was his, not mine. He spent forty years as a railroad man, raising and lowering gates at crossings, forty years as a signalman, forty years, like me, enjoying nothing but work, and when he retired he found he couldn't live without a signal tower, so he picked one up secondhand at a border station no longer in use and had it brought back to his garden, and then some of his friends who were retired engineers chipped in on a small locomotive—an Ohrenstein & Koppel that had once pulled skips and flatcars through a steelworks—and some tracks and three flatcars, all of which they found at a scrap heap somewhere, and once they'd laid the tracks in and around the trees of the old garden, they would stoke up the Ohrenstein & Koppel every Saturday and Sunday, and off they'd go, giving rides to children in the afternoon and—when evening came on and they began drinking beer and singing—rides to one another, or else they would all crowd together on the locomotive, and it would look like a statue of the river god Nile, the figure of a naked reclining Adonis dotted with figurines.

One day I went to see my uncle to find a place for my press, and as night fell, and the train, its lights aglow, rounded the apple- and pear-tree bends at top speed, I watched him sitting in his signal tower, busy at the switches and, to judge by the intermittently flashing aluminum tankard, every bit as well lubricated as the Ohrenstein & Koppel. Since I walked through the children's whoops and the old men's hoots without being invited to join in or asked whether I wanted a drink— they were all too involved in their games, which were really nothing more than the jobs they'd enjoyed all their lives—I simply kept walking, marked like Cain, and when, after walking on my own for an hour or so, I returned to see whether anyone would call me over, what I saw was that no one even recognized me, and when, after passing through the gate, I turned one last time, what I saw, by the light of the lanterns and the brightly lit signal tower, was a flurry of silhouettes and the train following them with a whistle and a clank on yet another journey along the crumpled ellipsis of its tracks, a hurdy-gurdy playing and replaying a single tune, a tune so catchy you never wanted to hear another as long as you lived. And even though no one could possibly have seen me from so far off, I could tell that my uncle saw me, that he had never taken his eyes off me all the time I was wandering through the trees, and he lifted his hand from the controls and waggled his fingers at me in an odd way, as if trying to make the air vibrate, and I waved back at him through the darkness, and we seemed to be saying good-bye from trains rushing in opposite directions.

When I reached the outskirts of Prague, I bought a sausage—and was I scared, because without raising it to my mouth I could feel it brushing my hot lips. And when I looked down—I was holding it at waist level— what did I see but the other end touching my shoes, but when I lifted it in both hands, it looked perfectly normal, so I knew I had shriveled up, shrunk, in the last ten years. When I got home, I pushed a couple of hundred books away from the kitchen door and found the lines I used to draw on the frame with an indelible pencil to show how tall I'd been on a given date, and I picked up a book, stepped back against the doorframe, and pressed the book flat on my head, and when I turned in place and drew another line there, I could tell with the naked eye that in eight years I had shrunk four inches, and I decided I must have shrunk under the weight of that two-ton canopy of books.

THREE

For thirty-five years now I've been compacting wastepaper, and if I had it all to do over I'd do just what I've done for the past thirty-five years. Even so, three or four times a year my job turns from plus to minus: the cellar suddenly goes bad, the nags and niggles and whines of my boss pound in my ears and head and make the room into an inferno; the wastepaper, piled to the ceiling, wet and moldy, ferments in a way that makes manure seem sweet, a swamp decomposing in the depths of my cellar, with bubbles rising to the surface like will-o'-the-wisps from a stump rotting in the mire. And I have to come up for air, get away from the press, but I never go out, I can't stand fresh air anymore, it makes me cough and choke and sputter like a Havana cigar. So while my boss is screaming and wringing his hands and raining threats down on me, I slip away and set off in search of other basements, other cellars.

Most of all I enjoy central-heating control rooms, where men with higher education, chained to their jobs like dogs to their kennels, write the history of their times as a sort of sociological survey and where I learned how the fourth estate was depopulated and the proletariat went from base to superstructure and how the university-trained elite now carries on its work. My best friends are two former members of our Academy of Sciences who have been set to work in the sewers, so they've decided to write a book about them, about their crissings and crossings under Prague, and they are the ones who taught me that the excrement entering the sewage plant at Podbaba on Sundays differs substantially from the excrement entering it on Mondays, and that each day is so clearly differentiated from the rest that the rate of flux may be plotted on a graph, and according to the ebb and flow of prophylactics one may determine the relative frequency with which varying sections of Prague indulge in sexual intercourse. Today, however, my friends made an even deeper impression on me with a report of a war, a total, humanlike war, between white rats and brown, which, though it ended in the absolute victory of the whites, had led to their immediate break-down into two groups, two opposing clans, two tightly organized rodent factions engaged at this very moment in a life-and-death struggle for supremacy of the sewers, a great rodent war over the rights to all the refuse and fecal matter flowing through the sewers to Podbaba, and as soon as the present war was over, my friends the academic sewersweeps informed me, the winning side would again break down, like gases and metals and all organic matter, into two dialectically opposed camps, the struggle for supremacy bringing life back to life, the desire for conflict resolution promising imminent equilibrium, the world never stumbling for an instant. I could see how right Rimbaud was when he wrote that the battle of the spirit is as terrible as any armed conflict; I could grasp the true meaning of Christ's cruel words, "I came not to send peace, but a sword"; and having received my education unwittingly, I was always amazed at Hegel and what he taught me, namely, that the only thing on earth worthy of fear is a situation that is petrified, congealed, or dying, and the only thing worthy of joy is a situation where not only the individual but also society as a whole wages a constant battle for self-justification.

Wandering through the streets of Prague on the way back to my cellar, I switched on my X-ray eyes and peered down through transparent pavements into the sewers to find rodent general staffs mapping out operations for rodent troops, generals barking orders into their walkie-talkies about which front to put pressure on, but I just kept walking, listening to the crunch of sharp little rats' teeth under my shoes and thinking of the melancholy of a world eternally under construction, and when I looked up through my tears I noticed something I had never noticed before, namely, that the façades, the fronts of all the buildings, public and residential—and I could see them all the way up to the drainpipes—were a reflection of everything Hegel and Goethe had dreamed of and aspired to, the Greece in us, the beautiful Hellenic model and goal. I saw Doric columns and frieze-covered gutters, I saw Corinthian columns with florid leafage, I saw Ionic columns with volutes and stately shafts, I saw garlanded cornices, templelike vestibules, caryatids and balustrades reaching to the roofs of the buildings—and I walked in their shadows. I had seen it all in the poorer sections of town, too, Greece plastered over the most ordinary buildings, their portals adorned with naked men and naked women and the boughs and buds of alien flora. Anyway, on I walked, thinking about what the boilerman with the university education had told me, that Eastern Europe doesn't start outside the gates of Prague, it starts at the last Empire-style railroad station somewhere in Galicia, at the outer limits of the Greek tympanum, and Prague's involvement with the Greek spirit goes deeper than the façades of its buildings, it goes straight into the heads of the populace, because classical gymnasia and humanistic universities have stuffed millions of Czech heads full of Greece and Rome. And while the sewers of Prague provide the scene for a senseless war between two armies of rats, the cellars are headquarters for Prague's fallen angels, university-educated men who have lost a battle they never fought, yet continue to work toward a clearer image of the world.

When I got back to my own cellar and saw my little mice hopping and skipping up to say hello, I thought of the hatch at the bottom of the elevator shaft and the sewer it kept at bay, and I climbed down the ladder to the bottom of the shaft, screwed up my courage, yanked off the cover, kneeled down, and listened to the whish of wastewater, the applause of toilets flushing, the melodic runoff from basins and once-soapy baths, a miniature seashore, as it were, but then I pricked up my ears and what did I hear sailing out over the waters but the whooping of warrior rats, the gnawing of meat, the keening, rejoicing, the lapping and gurgling of bodies in combat, sounds from a distance, yet I knew I could remove any gate or manhole cover in the city and climb straight down into the life-and-death struggle, the rat war to end all rat wars, and I knew it would end with a celebration lasting only till they could find a motive to start fighting again. I put the cover on and returned to my press, enriched by the new knowledge that there was a fierce battle going on under my feet, and if not even rat heaven was humane, then how could I be, I who have been baling wastepaper for thirty-five years and grown a little ratlike myself from living in cellars all that time. I don't like baths even though we have a shower room right behind the boss's office, because if I had a bath I'd be sure to come down with something. I have to go easy on the hygiene, working with my bare hands: I can't wash them until night, because if I washed them several times a day my skin would crack. But sometimes, when a yearning for the Greek ideal of beauty comes over me, I'll wash one of my feet or maybe even my neck, then the next week I'll wash the other foot and an arm, and whenever a major religious holiday is in the offing, I'll do my chest and both feet, but in that case I take an antihistamine in advance, because otherwise I'll have hay fever even if there's snow on the ground.

Now I'm back at my press, making up wastepaper bales, a classical philosopher in the heart of each bale, and my body is relaxed by my morning stroll through Prague, my mind is cleared by the thought that I am not alone, that there are thousands like me in Prague working underground, in basements and cellars, and that they have live, living, life-giving thoughts running through their heads. I have calmed down a little and my work is going better than yesterday, so well, in fact, that it does itself and I can slip back into the womb of time, into my youth, when I ironed my trousers and shined my shoes, soles included, every Saturday, because when you're young you love keeping clean, you love your self-image, an image you still have time to improve. Anyway, I would twirl my iron through the air until the hot coals spewed out sparks, lay the trousers on the ironing board—first smoothing out the buckled creases, then covering them with a cloth I'd squirted beforehand with a mouthful of water, and finally giving them a careful iron, especially the right leg, since it was always a little frayed from the habit I had of touching my knee to the dirt just before letting go of the ball in ninepins—and when at last I cautiously peeled off the hot, smoking cloth, I would hold my breath to see whether the creases were perfectly straight, because only then could I pull my trousers on and set off, as I did every Saturday, for the village square, where, just before I reached the log pile in front of the Lower Tavern, I would turn and see my mother watching, checking whether everything was as it should be and I looked my best.

It is evening, I'm at a dance, and in comes Marie (or Manča, as I call her), the girl I've been waiting for, ribbons trailing, ribbons braided in her hair, and the band plays and I dance only with her, we dance and the world swirls around us like a merry-go-round, and when out of the corner of my eye I look for an opening that Manča and I can polka into, I see Manča's ribbons swinging around me, borne straight out on the wind of the dance, and whenever I feel the need to slow down, the ribbons start to droop, but then I pick up again and whirl her around, and the ribbons pick up and graze my hands, the fingers that hold her hand, which holds on tightly to a white embroidered handkerchief, and for the first time I tell her I love her and she whispers back that she's loved me since school, and then all at once she presses against me, clasps me, and we're closer than we've ever been before, and she asks me to be her partner for Women's Choice, and I shout "Yes!" but no sooner does Women's Choice begin than Manča turns pale and tells me she'll only be a second.

When she came back, her hands were cold, but we started up again and I kept her twirling so everyone could see what a good dancer I was and how good we were together, what a couple we made, and as the polka reached its dizzy peak and Manča's ribbons started fluttering through the air with her straw-colored braid, I noticed the other couples had stopped dancing and were moving away from us in disgust, until finally they made a large ring around us, but not to admire us, no, to escape us, because centrifugal force was spraying them with something horrible, though exactly what it was neither Manča nor I could guess, until Manča's mother ran up, horror-stricken, grabbed her by the arm, and they ran out of the dance hall, out of the Lower Tavern, never to return, which meant that I didn't see her again for years. What had happened was that Manča was so excited by her Women's Choice, so thrilled by my I love you, that she had to pop out to the tavern latrine, where, unbeknownst to her, her ribbons had dipped into the pyramid of feces rising up to meet the board she sat on, and when she ran out into the brightly lit room and starting dancing, she splashed and splattered the dancers, every dancer within range, with the centrifugal force of her ribbons, and from that day on they called her Shithead Manča.

I compact wastepaper, and when I press the green button the wall of my press advances, and when I press the red button it retreats, thereby describing a basic motion of the world, like the bellows of a concertina, like a circle, which must return to its point of departure. Manča, having relinquished glory, was left with shame, which was not her doing, since what had happened was only too human: Goethe would have forgiven Ulrike von Levetzow the ribbon episode, Schelling would have forgiven his Karoline, but then again, Leibniz seems unlikely to have forgiven his royal mistress Sophie

Charlotte, to say nothing of the ultrasensitive Hölderlin and his Madame Gontard.

When five years later I tracked her down—the whole family had packed up and moved to Moravia to escape the ribbons—I asked her to forgive me, because I always feel I'm to blame for everything—anything that happens, anything I ever read about in the papers—and she forgave me, so I invited her to go on a trip with me, because I'd won five thousand crowns in a lottery and couldn't wait to see the last of them: I hate money, to say nothing of savings accounts. So off we went to the mountains, to the Hotel Renner on Golden Peak, a luxurious hotel that would be quick to part me from the money and the worries that go with it, and every night the guests outdid one another to woo Manča away from me, especially an industrialist by the name of Jína, but I was happy, because I was spending the money, spending it on anything our hearts desired. It was late February, the sun shone every day, and every day my beautifully tanned Manča went out skiing, flying down the sparkling slopes in a sleeveless, low-cut blouse, surrounded by men, while I sat sipping cognac, and whereas by noon all the men were back on the terrace in front of the hotel tanning themselves in a row of fifty chairs and chaise longues flanked by thirty small, aperitif-laden tables, Manča kept skiing until just before dinner, when she would suddenly glide up to the hotel. On our last day there, no, next-to-the-last, our fifth day, when all I had left was five hundred crowns, I was sitting in the row of guests watching Manča, tan and beautiful, flying down Golden Peak, I was sitting there clinking glasses with Mr. Jína, the industrialist, who took me for an industrialist, too, watching her vanish behind a clump of pines and scraggy spruces, then reappear, resume her rapid journey, and glide up to the hotel as usual. It was such a beautiful day and the sun was so warm that all the chairs and chaise longues were occupied, and one of the porters had to bring out more, and meanwhile my Manča promenaded up and down the row of tanning guests—Mr. Jína was right, she was as pretty as a picture that day—but as she passed the first sun worshipers I noticed the women turning after her and snickering into their hands, and the closer she came to me, the more women I saw stifling their laughter, the more men I saw falling back in their chairs and pulling their newspapers over their faces, pretending they had swooned or were seeking shelter from the sun, and when she glided up to me, what did I see on one of her skis, just behind the boot, but an enormous turd, a turd the size of the paperweight the poet Vrchlický celebrated in sublime verse, and then and there I knew we had come to the second chapter in the life of Manča, who, never having known glory, would never relinquish shame. Well, Mr. Jína, the businessman, took one look at the big business Manča had done on her ski behind a scraggy spruce in the foothills of Golden Peak and fainted dead away, and he was still quite pale that afternoon, by which time Manča's face was bright red to the roots of her hair. No, the heavens are not humane, nor is any man with a head on his shoulders.

Here I stand, compacting bale after bale, placing a book open to its finest passage in the heart of each, but as I work, my thoughts are with Manča, who helped me to drink up my last few crowns that night, though neither champagne nor cognac could erase the image of Manča's promenading her business in front of everyone. I spent the rest of the night begging her to forgive me for what had happened, but she refused, and early next morning she left the Hotel Renner, head held high, thereby confirming Lao-tze's dictum: Know thy shame and preserve thy glory. A shining example, that woman.

Opening the *Canonical Book of Virtues* to the proper page, I placed it like a priest on the altar of my press, which I had lined with greasy pastry paper and empty cement sacks. I pushed the green button, the press started churning like fingers clasping in a desperate prayer, and I watched it compact the *Canonical Book of Virtues*, the source of the associations leading me back to Manča, the beauty of my youth. From the tunnels, from the sewers, where two rat armies were locked in a life-and-death battle, came a whish of wastewater, a subterranean subtext. Today was a beautiful day.

FOUR

One afternoon the slaughterhouse people brought me a truckload of bloodstained paper and blood-drenched boxes, crate after crate of the stuff, which I couldn't stand, because it had that sickly sweet smell to it and left me as gory as a butcher's apron. By way of revenge I piously placed an open *Praise of Folly* by Erasmus of Rotterdam into the first bale, a *Don Carlos* by Friedrich Schiller into the second, and, that the word might be made bloody flesh, an *Ecce Homo* by Friedrich Nietzsche into the third. And as I worked, a host, a swarm of those dreadful flesh flies the butchers had brought with them from the slaughterhouse buzzed around my head, attacking my face like a hailstorm.

While I was on my fourth mug of beer, I noticed a pleasant-looking young man next to the press, and I knew then and there it was Jesus Himself. And soon he was joined by an old man with a face full of wrinkles, and I knew on the spot it could only be Lao-tze. So there they stood, side by side, the better for me to compare them, an elderly gentleman and a young man, as thousands of cobalt-colored flies swooped in thousands of wild nosedives, their metallic wings and bodies embroidering an immense *tableau vivant* made up of constantly shifting curves and splashes like the flow of paint in those gigantic Jackson Pollocks.

Not that I was surprised to find the two of them there: my grandfathers and great-grandfathers had visions too when they drank, but they saw fairy-tale characters. My grandfather met all kinds of mermaids and water nymphs in his wanderings, and my great-grandfather believed in the imps, sprites, and fairies he saw in the Litovel Brewery malthouse. As for me, with my unwitting education, when I lie falling asleep under my two-ton canopy of books, I see visions of Schelling and Hegel, who were born in the same year, and once Erasmus of Rotterdam rode up on his horse and asked me how to get to the sea. So I wasn't surprised when another two of my favorites showed up. Seeing them side by side, I realized for the first time how important their age was for an understanding of their teachings, and leaning through the flies' fandango in my wet, blood-soaked smock, I pushed first the green button, then the red button, and watched Jesus, an ardent young man intent on changing the world, rise up and take over Lao-tze's place at the summit, while the old man looked on submissively, using the return to the sources to line his eternity; I watched Jesus cast a spell of prayer on reality and lead it in the direction of miracle, while Lao-tze followed the laws of nature along the Tao, the only Way to learned ignorance. And all the while I was loading armfuls of wet, red paper and my face was smeared with blood. Then I pushed the green button, and the press started compacting the flies along with the disgusting paper, the flesh flies that couldn't tear themselves away from what was left of the meat and were mad for its odor and started rutting and mating, and as their passion drove them into wilder and wilder pirouettes, they formed thick orbits of dementia around the drum full of paper, like neutrons and protons swirling around their atoms.

Drinking from my mug, I kept my eyes glued to the young Jesus, all ardor amidst a group of youths and pretty girls, and the lonely Lao-tze, looking only for a worthy grave. Even as the compacting process reached its final stage and the paper started squirting and dripping blood and flesh-fly juice, I watched the young Jesus still suffused with mellow ecstasy and Lao-tze leaning sad and pensive against the edge of the drum and looking on with scornful indifference; I watched Jesus giving confident orders and making a mountain move, and Lao-tze spreading a net of ineffable intellect over the cellar; I watched Jesus the optimistic spiral and Lao-tze the closed circle, Jesus bristling with dramatic situations and Lao-tze lost in thought over the insolubility of moral conflicts.

When the red signal lit up and the bloodstained

wall started retreating, I went back to pitching boxes and cartons and blood-soaked wrappings into the drum, but I also found the strength to skim a book by Friedrich Nietzsche, or at least the pages about his cosmic friendship with Richard Wagner, before plunging it into the drum like a child into a bath, and just in time to swat away a swarm of blue and green flies lashing at my eyes like weeping-willow branches in a whirlpool. And the moment I pushed the green button, what should come tripping daintily down the cellar stairs but two skirts, one turquoise blue, the other velvet violet, the skirts of two Gypsy girls who always came as a revelation, visiting me when I least expected them, when I thought they'd died, their throats slit by a lover's knife. These two Gypsy girls, who collected wastepaper and lugged it around on their backs in huge bundles the way women carried grass from the woods in the old days, would waddle their loads along crowded streets, and people had to step aside for them and retreat into doorways, and their packs were so big that whenever they tried to come into our courtyard they clogged the entrance, but they'd squeeze through, make straight for the scale, bend over, turn, and fall into the pile of paper smack on their backs, only then undoing the straps and freeing themselves from their enormous yoke, after which they'd drag the bundle onto the scale and, wiping their sweaty foreheads, look up at the dial, which always showed at least seventy-five, and sometimes a hundred or a hundred and twenty-five pounds of boxes and cartons and refuse paper from various shops and distribution centers. And whenever they began to miss me or whenever their loads became too great—they were so strong and had so much energy that from a distance those bundles on their backs looked more like a small train or tram—they would come down and pay me a visit, throw off their canvas-covered burdens, fall back on their piles of dry paper, roll their skirts up to their belly buttons, pull out cigarettes and matches, and light up, flat on their backs, inhaling the smoke as if chomping on chocolate. I shouted a greeting, and, though surrounded by a cloud of flies, I could see the turquoise Gypsy lying on her back with her skirt up to her waist—fine legs and a fine naked stomach and a bush of hair surging up from below like a flame, one hand under the kerchief that held the dark, greasy hair together behind her neck, the other raising the cigarette to her mouth, oh, how innocent she looked—and the velvet-violet Gypsy lying like a tossed-off towel, exhausted, spent from her tyrannical labors. I pointed an elbow at my briefcase—I usually bought salami and bread on the way to work, then took it home with me, because I couldn't eat a thing when I drank, and I almost always drink at work, because I'm so excited, overwhelmed, overwrought—and the Gypsy girls rolled themselves out of the paper like two rocking chairs and, sticking their cigarettes in their mouths, lunged into the briefcase, four hands pulling out the salami, dividing it equally; and then, snuffing out the cigarettes with great theatricality, grinding them into the floor with their heels as if they were snake heads, they sat back down and set to. Only after they had polished off the salami did they start in on the bread—and how I loved to watch them eat it: suddenly very serious, they would crumble it with their fingers and raise each morsel separately to their mouths, nodding and touching shoulders like a team of horses pulling the dray to the knacker's, and in fact, if I came across the two of them in the street dragging their packs from shop to warehouse, they always had their arms around each other's waists and cigarettes in their mouths and they always walked in a kind of polka step. They had a hard time of it, those Gypsy girls: they had not only themselves and two children to support, they also had to support their man, a Gypsy who took his cut every afternoon according to the size of their bundles. He was a strange type, that Gypsy: he wore gold-rimmed glasses, had a mustache, and parted his hair down the middle, and I never saw him without a camera slung over his shoulder. He took their picture every day, posing them carefully and stepping back to frame the picture, while they flashed him the brightest of smiles, but he never had film in the camera and the Gypsy girls never saw a single shot of themselves, and still they had their picture taken every day and looked forward to the results like Christians to heaven.

One day I ran into my Gypsy girls on the other side of the Vltava where the Libeň Bridge swings over from Holešovice. As I was walking along, I noticed a Gypsy policeman with white sleeves and a striped stick directing traffic at the bend near Scholer's, and the way he polka-stepped to change the flow of traffic was so striking and dignified that I stopped to watch him finish his half-hour shift, and suddenly a flash of turquoise blue and a blaze of velvet violet caught my eye, and who did I see across the street but my two Gypsy girls—attracted like me by the sight of a Gypsy directing traffic at a busy intersection—in a crowd of Gypsy children and a few older Gypsies, all of them beaming with pride at the heights to which a Gypsy had risen. And when his time was up and he had passed the intersection on to his replacement, he went over to bask in the praise and congratulations of his fellow Gypsies, and all at once I saw the turquoise-blue and velvet-violet skirts fall to their knees and start shining the policeman's dusty shoes. At first the Gypsy merely smiled, but soon his joy got the better of him and he laughed and kissed all the Gypsy girls ceremoniously, while the turquoise-blue and velvet-violet skirts went on shining his shoes.

When they had finished the salami and bread, they picked the crumbs off their skirts and ate them too, and then the turquoise Gypsy stretched out in the paper and hitched up her skirt to the waist. "How about it, chief?" she said seriously. "You game?" I showed her my hands full of blood. "Not today," I said. "Got a bad knee." She shrugged and rolled down her turquoise skirt, staring at me the whole time with unblinking eyes, as the velvet-violet Gypsy had been doing from her perch on the bottom step. Then they both stood up, refreshed and invigorated, gathered the edges of their canvas sails, and, just before disappearing, dropped their heads between their legs like folding rulers, shouted their alto good-byes, and ran out into the corridor, and soon I could hear their feet pattering across the courtyard in their inimitable polka gait, moving on to new piles of wastepaper as per the orders of the finely combed and neatly parted Gypsy photographer with the gold-rimmed glasses.

So I went back to work, hacking away at the blood-soaked boxes, cartons, and wrapping paper, until they started cascading from ceiling to drum, and once the hole in the ceiling was free, I could hear everything going on in the courtyard, everything being said there, as if through a megaphone. Some of my regulars came up to the opening, and I peered up at them from below, and if they looked to me like statues on a church portal, my press looked to them like the catafalque of Charles IV, father of our country. Then suddenly they were replaced by my boss, wringing his hands and booming down at me in a voice full of malice, "Haňťa, what were those fortune-tellers, those witches, doing here again?" Trembling as usual, I dropped to one knee and, holding on to the drum with one hand, looked up, wondering what he, my boss, had against me, what made him pull such terrifying faces, faces so indignant, so full of suffering that they always made me believe that I was a repulsive person and a hopeless worker who inflicted the most ignoble blows on his noble superior.

I picked myself up from the floor as the terrified soldiers must have done when the stone covering the tomb where Christ lay buried sprang into the air and set Him free, I picked myself up, dusted off my knees, and went back to work. By then the flesh flies were out in full force, maybe because I'd stirred up a draft by clearing the hole in the ceiling; in any case, they formed a thick shrub around me and my hands—a raspberry bush, a bramble patch—and brushing them away was like forging a path through filings of iron wire, but soaked in blood and sweat though I was, I never stopped working.

While the Gypsy girls were with me, Jesus and Lao-tze had been standing together in the drum of my hydraulic press; now that I was alone again, wound in wires of flesh flies but left to my own devices and the routine of my work, I saw Jesus as a tennis champion who has just won his first Wimbledon and Lao-tze as a destitute merchant, I saw Jesus in the sanguine corporality of his ciphers and symbols and Lao-tze in a shroud, pointing at an unhewn plank; I saw Jesus as a playboy and Lao-tze as an old gland-abandoned bachelor; I saw Jesus raising an imperious arm to damn his enemies and Lao-tze lowering his arms like broken wings; I saw Jesus as a romantic, Lao-tze as a classicist, Jesus as the flow, Lao-tze as the ebb, Jesus as spring, Lao-tze as autumn, Jesus as the embodiment of love for one's neighbor, Lao-tze as the height of emptiness, Jesus as *progressus ad futurum*, Lao-tze as *regressus ad originem*.

Anyway, I went on pushing the green button and the red button until at last I'd thrown the final armful of repulsive bloodstained paper into the drum, cursing the butchers for cramming my cellar full of the stuff yet blessing them for bringing me Jesus and Lao-tze, so in the last bale I put a *Metaphysics of Morals* by Immanuel

Kant, and the flesh flies went berserk, attacking the last bits of dried and drying blood with such gluttony that they failed to notice the drum wall crushing and compacting them, separating them into membranes and cells. I fastened the compacted cube with wire and wheeled it out, surrounded by what was left of the still-crazed flies, to join the fourteen other bales, all of which were also strewn with flies, green or metallic-blue flies shining on every black-red drop of blood, each bale like a gigantic side of beef hanging from a hook in a provincial butcher's shop at hot high noon. I looked up and realized that Jesus and Lao-tze had disappeared up the white-washed stairs like the turquoise and velvet-violet skirts of my Gypsy girls before them, and looked down and realized that my pitcher was empty, so I stumbled up the stairs on all threes, my head spinning from too loud a solitude, and not until I'd made it to the back alley and breathed some fresh air in my lungs could I pick myself up and get a firm grip on the pitcher. The air was sparkling, the rays of the sun felt salty and made me blink, and as I walked along the wall of the Holy Trinity parish house, I saw those turquoise and velvet-violet skirts again: my Gypsy girls were sitting on a board, smoking and chatting with a group of Gypsy workers who were digging up the street. Lots of Gypsies work in road construction; they're paid by the job and they put their heart and soul into it, because having a goal keeps their energy up. I always like to watch them naked to the waist doing pickax battle with hard earth and cobblestones, I like to watch them underground to the waist seeming to dig their own graves, I like them because they keep their wives and children near the construction sites, and whenever one of them feels a yen for his baby, a Gypsy woman tucks up her skirt and takes over his pickax and he dandles the baby on his knee, and, oddly enough, playing with his baby seems to renew his strength, though not so much the strength in his arms as the strength in his soul. They're terribly sensitive people, the Gypsies, and like a beautiful Czech madonna playing with the infant Jesus they have big, human eyes that make your blood run cold, eyes that reflect the wisdom of a culture long forgotten. While we were running around with clubs in our hands and hides on our loins, the Gypsies had their own state and a social system that had been through two declines; and today's Gypsies, who have lived in Prague for only two generations, light a ritual fire wherever they work, a nomads' fire crackling only for the joy of it, a blaze of rough-hewn wood like a child's laugh, a symbol of the eternity that preceded human thought, a free fire, a gift from heaven, a living sign of the elements unnoticed by the world-weary pedestrian, a fire in the ditches of Prague warming the wanderer's eye and soul.

Eye, soul, and *hands*, when the weather's cold, I thought, entering Husenský's, and watched the barmaid pour four half-liter mugs down the inside wall of my pitcher and slide the rest across the counter for me to drink in a glass, because the foam had started running down the outside wall. Then she turned away fast, because when I paid the day before, a mouse had jumped out of my sleeve, or maybe it was my bloodstained hands, because when I stroke my face with my hand—I have a habit of stroking my face with an open hand—I splatter my forehead with the squashed fresh flies I smacked in self-defense. Anyway, as I walked back through the dug-up alley deep in thought, I saw the turquoise and velvet-violet skirts sparkling in the sun against the wall of Holy Trinity and watched the Gypsy with the camera pose their chins, step back, peer through the viewfinder, do whatever it took to make their rotogravure faces break out into happy smiles, and finally, the viewfinder pressed to his eye and his left hand raised in a wave, click the shutter and wind the nonexistent film; I watched the Gypsy girls clap with glee like children wondering how the pictures would come out.

Then I pulled my hat over my eyes and crossed the street to where a lost-looking philosophy professor stood aiming his thick, ashtray glasses at me as if they were a double-barreled shotgun. As usual he rummaged awhile in his pocket and came up with a ten-crown note, which he handed to me and asked, "Is the young man in?" And when I said he was, he whispered into my ear as usual, "You be nice to him, you hear?" And when I said I would, he slipped into our courtyard from the Spálená Street entrance, and I crossed over and ran around to the back and was down the stairs and hatless by the time I heard him making his timorous way across the courtyard and coming noiselessly down the stairs, and when our eyes met, he sighed and asked, "Where's the old man?" And as usual I said, "He's off somewhere having a beer." And the professor asked, "Does he still treat you like a brute?" And I said, as usual, "He's jealous, jealous because I'm younger than he is." And the philosophy professor gave me another crumpled ten-crown note, pressed it into my hand and, his voice quivering, said, "This is for you, to help you look. Have you found anything?" And I went over to a box and pulled out some back issues of *National Politics* and *National News*, and as usual they had theater reviews in them, articles written by Miroslav Rutte and Karel Engelmüller, so I gave them to the professor, who used to work at *Theater News*, and even though he'd been dismissed from the editorial board five years ago for political reasons, he still had a passion for theater reviews from the thirties. He gave them the once-over, stuffed them into his briefcase, and said good-bye, at which point, as usual, he slipped me another ten-crown note. Then, on the stairs, he turned and said, "Keep it up, keep looking! I just hope I don't run into the old man," and hurried out into the courtyard. Meanwhile, as usual, I threw my hat back on, ran out the back way into the alley and across the presbytery courtyard, and took up my post at the statue of Saint Thaddeus, my hat pulled down over my eyebrows and a look of grim surprise on my face, and I watched the philosophy professor sneak along the parish-house wall, watched him panic, as usual, when he saw me, but as soon as he recovered, he came up to me and, as usual, handed me a ten-crown note and said, "Don't be so hard on the young man. What have you got against him? You *will* be kind to him now, won't you?" And when, as usual, I nodded, he darted off, not going straight ahead to Charles Square, as I knew he should, but turning at the first corner, his briefcase flying behind him, in his haste to leave the old man who treated his young helper like dirt.

Just then I saw a truck backing into our courtyard, so I slipped down to the cellar and stood by the fifteen bales I had compacted today, all of them decorated with blood-speckled reproductions of Paul Gauguin's *Bonjour, M. Gauguin*, all of them shiny and bright, and I was sorry the driver had come so early: I'd have liked to spend more time with the pictures, layered as they were like stage sets, forming a beautiful if confusing backdrop for the droning flesh flies. But there was the driver's face leaning out of the elevator, so I loaded one bale after another on the dolly, feasting my eyes on the *Bonjour, M. Gauguin*s, sorry to see them go. Not that it matters, I said to myself, because when I'm retired and buy my press, I'll keep all the bales I make, even if somebody buys one of my signed bales, even a foreigner—but with my luck I'll mark it up to a thousand deutsch marks to put it out of reach and that foreigner will fork out a thousand deutsch marks and haul it away and I'll never be able to go and visit it again. Anyway, as bale after bale was hauled up to the courtyard, I heard the janitor cursing the flesh flies on and around them, and, sure enough, when the last bale vanished up the shaft, the flies all vanished with them. But without the flies the cellar suddenly seemed sad and downcast, so I crawled up the stairs—by the time I've drunk my fifth mug, I have to negotiate stairs like ladders—and saw the janitor placing the last bale into the driver's gloved hands and the driver hoisting it onto the truck with his knee, saw the back of the janitor's overalls smeared with a blood batik, saw the driver tear off his bloodstained gloves and fling them away in disgust, the janitor climb in next to the driver, and the bales pull out of the courtyard. I was glad the *Bonjour, M. Gauguin* sides showed above the slats, and I hoped that everyone the truck passed would enjoy it. As the truck drove off, the flesh flies came alive in the Spálená Street sun, swarms of blue, green, and gold flesh flies that were certainly entitled to be locked up with Paul Gauguin's *Bonjour, M. Gauguin*, in large crates and doused with acids and alkalis in paper mills, because those wild flies refuse to give up the idea that life is at its most beautiful in gloriously rancid, decomposing blood.

I was about to go back to the cellar when my boss dropped to his knees before me with a martyred look on his face and clasped his hands and pleaded, "Please, Haňt'a, for the love of God, come to your senses while there's still time and stop pouring those pitchers of beer down your gullet. Do your job and stop torturing us. You'll be the end of me if you go on like this." Trembling, I leaned over him and took him gently by the elbow. "Get a grip on yourself, my good man," I told him. "It's not dignified to kneel." And as I helped him up, I felt him shake all over, so I asked him to forgive me, without knowing what for, but that was my lot, asking forgiveness, I even asked forgiveness of myself for being what I was, what it was my nature to be.

Depressed, burdened with guilt, I made my way down to the cellar and lay on my back in the hollow still warm from the Gypsy girl in the turquoise skirt, I lay there listening to the sounds of the street, the beautiful concrete music of the street, and the dripping and flushing of wastewater that was constantly running through the five-story building above us, to toilet chains being pulled, listening to what was going on below, clearly hearing the far-off flow of wastewater and feces through the sewers, and far beneath the surface—now that the flesh flies' legions had beat a fast retreat—the keening and mournful squeaking of the two armies of rats battling throughout the sewers of the capital, battling for supremacy over the sewers of Prague. Neither the heavens are humane nor is life above or below—or within me. *Bonjour, M. Gauguin!*

FIVE

And so everything I see in this world, it all moves backward and forward at the same time, like a blacksmith's bellows, like everything in my press, turning into its opposite at the command of red and green buttons, and that's what makes the world go round. I've been compacting wastepaper for thirty-five years, a job that ought to require not only a good classical education, preferably on the university level, but also a divinity degree, because in my profession spiral and circle come together and *progressus ad futurum* meets *regressus ad originem*, and I experience it all firsthand: I, unhappily happy with my unwitting education, ruminate on *progressus ad futurum* meeting *regressus ad originem* for relaxation, the way some people read the *Prague Evening News*.

Yesterday we buried my uncle. He was the bard who

showed me the way by setting up a signal tower in his garden and laying tracks in and around the trees for an old Ohrenstein & Koppel locomotive he and his friends had put back in running order and stoked up every Saturday and Sunday afternoon to give children rides on the three flatcars and then go for rides themselves and drink beer by the tankard. Yesterday we buried my uncle, who had a stroke on the job, in his signal tower. It's the height of summer and his friends are all off in the woods and streams; he lay there on the signal-tower floor for two hot weeks before one of the engineers found him coated with flies and worms, his body running over the linoleum like an overripe Camembert. The undertakers picked up what had stuck to his clothes, then came and told me what had happened, and I went and got a shovel and trowel and scooped him bit by bit off the floor, fortified by a bottle of rum the undertakers had given me. Humbly and quietly I scraped up the remains of his remains, the toughest part being the red hair in the linoleum—it was like the spines of a porcupine run over by a truck; I had to use a chisel on it—and when I finished, I stuffed the leftovers under the clothes he had on in the coffin, covered his head with the cap I'd found hanging in the signal tower, and placed a volume of Immanuel Kant in his hands, opening it to a beautiful text that has never failed to move me: "Two things fill my mind with ever new and increasing wonder—the starry firmament above me and the moral law within me," but, changing my mind, I leafed through the younger Kant and found an even more beautiful passage:

"When the tremulous radiance of a summer night fills with twinkling stars and the moon itself is full, I am slowly drawn into a state of enhanced sensitivity made of friendship and disdain for the world and eternity." And when I opened his closet, there it was—the scrap-metal collection my uncle used to show me all the time, not that I'd ever appreciated it, a collection of metal of every possible color, boxes full, odds and ends of copper and brass and tin and iron and other colored metal he would lay out on the tracks when he was on duty, and every evening, after the train passed, he picked up and sorted them according to the wild shapes they had assumed, giving each piece a name by association with its shape and each box a motif, like Asian butterflies or chocolate-nougat foil wrappers. It wasn't until I'd taken one box after another and emptied them into my uncle's coffin, inundating him with his precious scrap-metal collection, that I let the undertakers put the lid on. There he lay, covered with medals, medallions, and orders, decked out like a dignitary, like a prize bale I had composed and compacted.

Then I went back to my cellar, crawling down the stairs backward, as if climbing down a ladder from the attic, and after quietly polishing off the bottle of rum and downing a beer chaser, I pickaxed my way through a mass of foul, sticky paper full of mice-made Swiss-cheese-like holes, and I after another drink of beer I forked it into my drum, mouse paths and all, whole nests full of mice, because we'd been closed for two days to give me time to make a clean sweep of the cellar before inventory. Hosing down the day's pile of wastepaper every evening, I never thought of what was going on at the very bottom of it all, at the bottom of the flowers and books and miscellaneous paper welded together by the mountain of waste resting on top of it and compacted as surely as if by my hydraulic press. As I say, it's a job for a theologian, because at the base, the bottom of the pile, a spot I hadn't got to for the six months since the last inventory, the wastepaper had rotted like roots in a swamp, giving off the sickly sweet stink of a cheese forgotten for months in the pantry, looking a dull, gray-beige mass with the consistency of stale bread. I worked well into the night, my only breaks being short trips to the air shaft, where I gazed up five stories like the young Kant at a piece of the starry firmament, and whence I crawled out the back way on all fours, pitcher in mouth, to return on all threes, pitcher in hand, backward, as if climbing down a ladder.

There, on the table under the light bulb, my copy of Immanuel Kant's *Theory of the Heavens* lay waiting, and over by the elevator my bales stood at attention, and because today I'd started in on a hundred large, soaking-wet reproductions of Vincent van Gogh's *Sunflowers*, the sides of each bale glowed gold and orange on a field of blue, making the smell of compacted mice and mouse nests and decomposing paper a bit more bearable. Meanwhile, the wall kept advancing and retreating, according to whether I pushed green or red, and in between I learned from the *Theory of the Heavens* how in the silence, the absolute silence of the night, when the senses lie dormant, an immortal spirit speaks in a nameless tongue of things that can be grasped but not described. And these lines so shocked me that I ran out to the air shaft and gazed up at my starry patch of firmament, but then I went back to forking foul paper and mouse families into my drum, and although anyone who compacts wastepaper for a living is no more humane than the heavens, somebody's got to do it, that slaying of the newborn as depicted by Pieter Brueghel, with which I happened to have wrapped all my bales last week. As for van Gogh's whorls and bull's-eyes of yellow and gold, they only intensified my tragic mood, but even so, I kept working and decorating mouse graves and running out to the shaft and reading the *Theory of the Heavens* a sentence at a time, savoring each sentence like a cough drop and brimming with a sense of the immensity, grandeur, and infinite beauty streaming at me from all sides, the starry firmament through the hole in the shaft above and the war between the two rat armies in the Prague sewers below. Meanwhile, the wall was lined with twenty bales, a twenty-car convoy on its way to the service elevator, each lit with sunflower light, and I still had a drum full of mashed mice which, like the mice caugₜt for fun by Cruel Tom Cat, never had a chance to squeak, merciful nature having come up with a horror destroying all sense of security, a horror more intense than pain, and visited it upon them in the moment of truth. It never ceased to amaze me, until suddenly one day I felt beautiful and holy for having had the courage to hold on to my sanity after all I'd seen and been through, body and soul, in too loud a solitude, and slowly I came to the realization that my work was hurtling me headlong into an infinite field of omnipotence.

The bulb kept shining down on me, the red and green buttons kept moving the wall back and forth, and at last I reached the bottom of the pile, using my knee, like a construction worker shoveling dirt, for leverage on the bottom's clayey, limestonelike layer. Slinging the last, viscous shovelful into the drum, I imagined myself a sewersweep cleaning out the basin of an abandoned underground canal. I opened the *Theory of the Heavens* and placed it in the last bale, and after winding the bale around with wire, loading it on the dolly, and rolling it over to the others, I sat on a step and let my arms hang down between my legs to the cold concrete floor. Twenty-one sunflowers lit up the dark cellar and the few mice left shivering for want of paper, and one mouse came up and attacked me, jumping on its hind legs and trying to bite me or knock me over, straining its tiny body, leaping at my leg and gnawing at my wet soles, and each time I brushed it away, gently, it would fling itself at my shoe until finally it ran out of breath and sat in a corner staring at me, staring me right in the eye, and all at once I started trembling, because in that mouse's eyes I saw something more than the starry firmament above me or the moral law within me. Like a flash of lightning Arthur Schopenhauer appeared to me and said, "The highest law is love, the love that is compassion," and I realized why Arthur hated strongman Hegel, and

I was glad that Hegel and Schopenhauer weren't leading opposing armies, because the two of them would wage the same war as those two rat armies in the sewers of Prague.

I was so worn out when I got home that I lay down on my bed fully dressed, and lying there crosswise under the canopy of shelves holding two tons of books, I looked up through the dim light coming from the street and through the cracks in the shelves, and when everything was perfectly silent I began to hear the gnawing of mouse teeth, hear them working away on the books in my heaven, and their ticking sound terrified me, because it was only a matter of time before they made a nest, and a few months after mice make nests they found a settlement, and six months later they form whole villages, which in geometric progression grow together within a year to make a city, a city of mice capable of gnawing through boards and beams with such skill that before long—yes, the time was not far off—it would take no more than a loud voice or a careless touch for the whole two tons of books to come down on my head and wreak vengeance on me for all the bales I've compacted the mice into. Anyway, there I lay, half asleep, overwhelmed by the gnawing going on above me, and, as usual when I drift off, I was joined by a tiny Gypsy girl in the form of the Milky Way, the quiet, innocent Gypsy girl who was the love of my youth and used to wait for me with one foot slightly forward and off to the side, like a ballet dancer in one of the positions, the beautiful, long-forgotten beauty of my youth.

Her body was covered with sweat and a gamey musk-and-pomade-scented grease that coated my fingers when I stroked her, and she always wore the same dress covered with soup and gravy stains in the front and whitewash and woodworm stains—from carrying rotten boards she found among the rubble—in the back. I met her near the end of the war when, on my way home from Horký's, where I'd had a few beers, she latched onto me, tagged along, so that I had to turn and talk to her over my shoulder, and she never tried to pass me, she just toddled noiselessly behind, and when we came to the first intersection I said, "Well, good-bye, I've got to be going," but she said she was going in the same direction, and when we got to the end of Ludmila Street I said, "Well, good-bye, I've got to be going home," and she said she was going in the same direction, so on we went, and I purposely walked all the way to Sacrifice and held out my hand to her and said, "I've got to be going home now," but she said she was going in the same direction, and on we went until we came to the Dam of Eternity, and I said I was home now and we'd have to say good-bye, and when I stopped at the gas lamp in front of my door and said, "Well, good-bye now, this is where I live," she said she lived there, too, so I unlocked the door and motioned for her to go in ahead of me, but she refused and told me to go in first, and since the hall was dark, I did, and then I went down the stairs and into the yard and up to the door of my room, and when I'd unlocked it, I turned and said, "Well, good-bye, this is my room," and she said it was her room, too, and she came in and shared my bed with me, and when I woke up in a bed still warm with her, she was gone. But the next day, and every day thereafter, the moment I set foot in the yard I saw her sitting on the steps in front of my door and some white boards and sawed-off beams lying under the window, and when I unlocked the door, she would leap up like a cat and scamper into my room, neither of us saying a word. Then I went for beer with my big, five-liter pitcher, and the Gypsy girl would light the old cast-iron stove, which boomed even with the door open, because the room had once been a blacksmith's shop and had a high ceiling and a huge fireplace, and she would make supper, which was always the same potato goulash with horse salami, then sit by the stove, feeding it with wood, and it was so hot that her lap glowed gold and gold sweat covered her hands, neck, and constantly changing profile, while I lay on the bed, getting up only to quench my thirst from the pitcher, after which I handed it to her, and she would hold the giant pitcher in both hands and drink in such a way that I heard her throat move, heard it moaning quietly like a pump in the distance. At first I thought she put so much wood on the fire just to win me over, but then I realized it was in her, the fire was in her, she couldn't live without fire.

So we went on living together even though I never really knew her name and she never knew or wanted or needed to know mine; we went on meeting every night, even though I never gave her the keys and sometimes stayed out late, until midnight, but the moment I unlocked the main door I would see a shadow slip past, and there she was, striking a match, setting fire to some paper, and a flame would sputter and flare in the stove, which she kept going with the month's supply of wood she'd laid in under the window. And later in the evening, while we ate our silent supper, I would turn on the light bulb and watch her break her bread as if she were taking Communion and gather up all the crumbs from her dress and toss them reverently into the fire. Then we switched off the bulb and lay on our backs, looking up at the ceiling and the shimmer of shadow and light, and the trip to the pitcher on the table was like wading through an aquarium filled with algae and other marine flora or stalking through a thick wood on a moonlit night, and as I drank I always turned and looked at my naked Gypsy girl lying there looking back at me, the whites of her eyes glowing in the dark—we looked at each other more in the dark than by the light of day. I always loved twilight: it was the only time I had the feeling that something important could happen. All things were more beautiful bathed in twilight, all streets, all squares, and all the people walking through them; I even had the feeling that *I* was a handsome young man, and I liked looking at myself in the mirror, watching myself in the shop windows as I strode along, and even when I touched my face, I felt no wrinkles at my mouth or forehead. Yes, with twilight comes beauty. By the flames in the stove's open door the Gypsy girl stood up, naked, and as she moved, I saw her body outlined in a yellow halo like the halo emanating from the Ignatius of Loyola cemented to the façade of the church in Charles Square, and when she added some wood to the fire and came back and lay down on top of me, she turned her head to have a look at my profile and ran her finger around my nose and mouth. She hardly ever kissed me, nor I her; we said everything with our hands and then lay there looking at the sparks and flickers in the battered old cast-iron stove, curls of light from the death of wood. All we wanted was to go on living like that forever. It was as if we had said everything there was to say to each other, as if we had been born together and never parted.

During the last autumn of the war I bought some blue wrapping paper, a ball of twine, and glue, and while the Gypsy girl kept my glass filled with beer, I spent a whole Sunday on the floor making a kite, balancing it carefully so it would rise, and I tacked on a long tail of tiny paper doves strung together by the Gypsy girl under my tutelage, and then we went up to Round Bluff, and after flinging the kite to the heavens and letting the cord run free for a while, I held it back and gave it a few tugs to make it straighten up and stand motionless in the sky so that only the tail rippled, S-like, and the Gypsy girl covered her face to her eyes, eyes wide with amazement. Then we sat down and I handed it to her, but she cried out that it would carry her up to heaven—she could feel herself ascending like the Virgin Mary—so I put my hands on her shoulders and said if that was the case we'd go together, but she gave me back the ball of twine and we just sat there, her head on my shoulder, and suddenly I got the idea to send a message, and handed the kite to the Gypsy girl again, but again she froze and said it would fly away with her and she'd never see me again, so I pushed the stick with the twine into the ground, tore a page out of my memo pad, and attached it to the tail, and as soon as the twine was back in my hands, she started screaming and reaching after the message as it jerked its way up to the sky, each burst of wind traveling through my fingers to my whole body, I even felt the message making contact with the tip of the kite, and suddenly I shuddered all over, because suddenly the kite was God and I was the Son of God, and the cord was the Holy Spirit which puts man in contact, in dialogue with God. And once we'd flown the kite a few more times, the Gypsy girl screwed up her courage and took over the twine—trembling as I had trembled, trembling to see the kite tremble in the gusty wind—and, winding the twine around her finger, she cried out in rapture.

One evening I came home to find her gone. I switched on my light and went back and forth to the street until morning, but she didn't come, not that day or the next or ever again, though I looked everywhere for her. My childlike little Gypsy, simple as unworked wood, as the breath of the Holy Spirit—all she ever wanted was to feed the stove with the big, heavy boards and beams she brought on her back, crosslike, from the rubble, all she ever wanted was to make potato goulash with horse salami, feed her fire with wood, and fly autumn kites. Later I learned that she had been picked up by the Gestapo and sent with a group of Gypsies to a concentration camp, and whether she was burned to death at Majdanek or asphyxiated in an Auschwitz gas chamber, she never returned. The heavens are not humane, but I still was at the time. When she failed to return at the end of the war, I burned the kite and twine and the long tail she had decorated, a tiny Gypsy girl whose name I'd never quite known.

Well into the fifties my cellar was piled high with Nazi literature, and there was nothing I enjoyed more than compacting tons of Nazi pamphlets and booklets, hundreds of thousands of pages with pictures of cheering men, women, and children, cheering graybeards, cheering workers, cheering peasants, cheering SS men, cheering soldiers. I got a specially big kick out of loading my drum with Hitler and his entourage entering liberated Danzig, Hitler entering liberated Warsaw, Hitler entering liberated Prague, Hitler entering liberated Vienna, Hitler entering liberated Paris, Hitler at home, Hitler at harvest festivals, Hitler with his faithful sheepdog, Hitler visiting his troops at the front, Hitler inspecting the Atlantic Wall, Hitler en route to the conquered towns of East and West, Hitler leaning over military maps. And the more I compacted the cheering men, women, and children, the more I thought of my Gypsy girl, who had never cheered, who had wanted nothing more than to feed the fire, make her potato goulash, and fill my large pitcher with beer, nothing more than to break her bread like the wafer at Communion and look into the stove door, transfixed by the flames and heat and noise of the fire, the song of the fire, which she had known since childhood and which held sacred ties to her people. It left all pain behind and coaxed a melancholy smile to her face, a reflection of perfect happiness.

Now I am lying in bed crosswise, on my back, and a tiny mouse has just fallen on my chest, slid down to the floor, and scurried for shelter under the bed. I've probably brought home a few mice in my briefcase or coat pocket as well. A toilet-scented perfume drifts up from the yard: we're in for some rain, I tell myself. I'm so worn out from work and beer that I can't move a finger—two whole days of cleaning the cellar at the cost of those humble little creatures that wanted nothing more than to nibble at a few old books and live in wastepaper holes, give birth to other mice and feed them in cozy nests, tiny mice rolled into balls the way my tiny Gypsy rolled into a ball next to me on cold nights. The heavens are not humane, but I'd forgotten compassion and love.

S I X

For thirty-five years now I've compacted wastepaper in a hydraulic press, for thirty-five years I thought there was no other way, but then I began hearing about a new press over in Bubny, a gigantic press that did the work of twenty, and when eyewitnesses reported it made bales of seven and eight hundred pounds, bales delivered directly to the train by forklift, I said to myself, "This is something you've got to see, Hań'a, with your own eyes. It's time for a courtesy call." And when I got to Bubny and saw the enormous glass structure and heard the press booming away, I was so shaken I couldn't look at the machine, I just stood there and turned my head away, fumbled with my shoelaces—anything to keep from looking that machine in the face.

To peer into the mass of wastepaper and find the spine and boards of a rare book has always been a special treat for me. Instead of going after it on the spot, I'll take a piece of steel wool and give the shaft a good rub, then have another look at the paper and check whether I have the strength to pull out the book and open it, and not until I decide I do have the strength will I pick it up, and even then it shakes in my hands like a bride's bouquet at the altar. That's the way it was in the old days, too, when I played soccer for the village club: I knew the lineup wasn't posted in the Lower Tavern until Thursday, but I would ride down on Wednesdays, my heart thumping, and stand there astride my bike scrutinizing the notice board itself—the lock, the glass case—unable to look directly at the notice, then I'd read out the name of our club, letter by letter, and only then glance at the lineup, but since it was Wednesday the lineup was still the previous week's, so off I rode, to return the next day, when again I would stand there astride my bike scrutinizing everything but the lineup, and once I took hold of myself, I would read slowly down the lineup of the first team, slowly down the lineup of the second team, and slowly down the lineup of the juniors, and not until I found my name among the substitutes was I happy again.

Standing in front of the gigantic press at Bubny, I had the same feeling, and once I was over the initial shock, I took hold of myself and glanced at the machine, which rose up to the glass roof like the gigantic altar at St. Nicholas in Prague. It was even bigger than I had expected, with a conveyor belt as long and wide as the one that slowly dumps coal under the grates at the Holešovice Power Station, but what was slowly moving along this belt was books, books put there by young workers in getups quite different from what I or others like me wore at work: they were wearing orange and baby-blue gloves and yellow American baseball caps, and overalls that went up to their chests, and suspenders that went over their shoulders and crossed on their backs and showed off the T-shirts and turtlenecks they had on underneath. And nowhere did I see a light bulb: sunlight streamed in through the glass walls and glass ceiling, and the ceiling had a ventilation system to boot. But it was the gloves that got my goat: I always worked with my bare hands, I loved the feel of the paper in my fingers, but nobody here had the slightest desire to experience the palpable charm of wastepaper, and the conveyor belt moved the books and some miscellaneous scraps of white paper just as the Wenceslas Square escalator moves people up into the street, and that paper went straight into an enormous drum, a drum as big as the cauldron used for brewing at the Smíchov Brewery, and when the drum was full, the conveyor belt turned itself off and a propellerlike contraption descended from the ceiling, forced its mammoth strength on the paper, and with a magnificent snort returned to the ceiling, whereupon the conveyor belt jerked new books into motion and on to the oval drum as big as the fountain in Charles Square. By now I had calmed down enough to realize that the machine compacted and baled whole runs of books, and through the glass wall I could see trucks pulling up with boxes of books piled to the brim, the entire printing of a book going straight into the pulper before a single page could be sullied by the human eye, brain, or heart. Only now did I see the workers at the foot of the conveyor belt tearing open the boxes, taking the virgin books out of them, pulling the covers off, and tossing the naked insides on the belt, and it didn't matter what page they fell open to: nobody ever looked into them, nobody even dreamed of looking into them, because whereas I stopped my press all the time, they had to keep the belt full and moving. It was inhuman, the work they were doing in Bubny; it was like work on a trawler, when the nets are hauled in and the crew sort big fish from small, tossing them on belts that go directly to canning machines in the bowels of the ship: one fish after another, one book after another.

Plucking up my courage, I climbed the steps to the platform that ran around the oval drum, and as I walked along it, imagining myself in the brewing room at Smíchov, where they brew five hundred hectoliters of beer at once, or on the second-story scaffolding of a house under repair, I looked down and saw the control panel with all its colored buttons and the propeller mashing the contents of the drum the way you mash a ticket in your fingers when you're not thinking about it, and I was so scared I looked this way and that, and what I saw was workers bathed in glass-wall sun, their overalls and T-shirts and caps lost in a riot of color, like exotic birds they were, like kingfishers, Norwegian bullfinches, like parrots. But that wasn't what scared me; what scared me was that suddenly I knew for certain that the gigantic press before me was sounding the knell of all smaller presses, I saw that all this meant a new era in my specialty, that these people were different and their habits different. Gone were the days of small joys, of finds, of books thrown away by mistake: these people represented a new way of thinking. Even if each of the workers took home one book from each printing as payment in kind, it wouldn't be the same, it would still be the end of us, the old guard, because we were all educated unwittingly: each of us had a decent home library of books we'd happened to rescue, and each of us read those books in the blissful hope of making a change in his life. But the biggest shock came when I saw the young workers shamelessly guzzling milk and soft drinks—legs spread wide, hand on hip—straight from the bottle. Then I knew the good old days had come to an end, the days when a worker shoveled in his own wastepaper, went down on his knees in one-on-one combat, and ended each day filthy and exhausted from the effort. This was a new era with new men and new methods—think of drinking *milk* at work, when everyone knows that even a cow would rather die of thirst than touch a drop of the stuff! I couldn't take any more, so I circled the press to have a look at the fruit of its labor, a single titanic bale the size of a rich family's mausoleum, the size of a Wertheim safe, and saw it descend onto the platform of the lizardlike forklift, which jerked its way around and out to a ramp leading straight to a freight car. I put my head in my hands—dirty human hands with fingers gnarled like vines by work—but soon dropped them in disgust and watched my arms swing from the shoulders.

Just then the noon break began and the conveyor belt stopped and the workers sat down under a large board with all kinds of notices and announcements pinned on it, and each worker took out a bottle of milk and unpacked the lunch delivered by the lunch woman, and while they sat there laughing and chatting and slowly washing down their salami and cheese and buttered rolls with milk and soft drinks, I stood clinging to the railing, afraid of toppling over from the bits and pieces of conversation I overheard. It turned out that they were a Brigade of Socialist Labor, and every Friday the factory sent a bus to take them to the factory chalet in the Krkonoše Mountains, and last year they'd gone on a tour of France and Italy and this year they were going to Bulgaria and Greece. After watching them collect names for the Balkan tour and talk one another into signing up, I wasn't the least bit surprised to see them strip half naked to take advantage of the rays of the sun, now high in the sky, and hear them discuss how to make the most of that afternoon—whether to go for a swim in the river or have a game of soccer.

That Greek holiday of theirs gave me a real jolt: I had dreamed myself to Greece by reading Herder and Hegel, I had developed a Dionysian concept of the world by reading Friedrich Nietzsche, but I had never been on a holiday; I had to spend nearly all my time off making up days missed—my boss deducted two days for every unexcused absence—and if I did have a day left over,

I'd work for the extra pay, because I was always behind, there were always mounds of paper in the cellar and in the courtyard, more paper than I could get to. So for thirty-five years I'd lived with, lived through, a daily Sisyphus complex, the kind so beautifully described for me by Messrs. Sartre and Camus, especially the latter: the more bales driven out of my courtyard, the more wastepaper filled my cellar, whereas the Brigade of Socialist Labor at Bubny was always on schedule. Now they were back at work, nicely tanned, the sun deepening the hue of their Grecian bodies even as they toiled, not at all upset at the thought of going to Hellas knowing next to nothing about Aristotle or Plato or even Goethe, that extension of ancient Greece, no, they just went on working, pulling covers off books and tossing the bristling, horrified pages on the conveyor belt with the utmost calm and indifference, with no feeling for what the book might mean, no thought that somebody had to write the book, somebody had to edit it, somebody had to design it, somebody had to set it, somebody had to proofread it, somebody had to make the corrections, somebody had to read the galley proofs, and somebody had to check the page proofs, print the book, and somebody had to bind the book, and somebody had to pack the books into boxes, and somebody had to do the accounts, and somebody had to decide that the book was unfit to read, and somebody had to order it pulped, and somebody had to put all the books in storage, and somebody had to load them onto the truck, and somebody had to drive the truck here, where workers wearing orange and baby-blue gloves tore out the books' innards and tossed them onto the conveyor belt, which silently, inexorably jerked the bristling pages off to the gigantic press to turn them into bales, which went on to the paper mill to become innocent, white, immaculately letter-free paper, which eventually would be made into other, new, books.

And as I stood there, leaning on the railing and watching the work going on below me, a group of children with their teacher appeared in the sunlight, a school trip, I guessed, a chance for the children to see how wastepaper is recycled, and then the teacher picked up a book, called her pupils' attention to it, and demonstrated how it was torn apart, after which all her pupils, one after the other, picked up books, discarded the jackets, and started tearing them apart, and even though their fingers were small and the books put up a good deal of resistance, the fingers won out, and soon the children's foreheads smoothed over, and their work, encouraged by an occasional hand-wave from the Brigade, proceeded without a hitch. It reminded me of the time I visited the poultry farm in Libuš and saw young girls pulling out the innards of chickens hung up live on a conveyor belt, working with the same deft motions the children used to pull out the innards of the books, tossing livers, lungs, and hearts into the proper buckets, while the belt carried the twitching chickens off for further operations, and what struck me most as I looked on was that all those girls in Libuš could be cheerful and gay doing what they were doing and doing it in the midst of a thousand cages with ten half-dead chickens in each cage plus a few escapees waddling around or pecking but never thinking to fly away from the hooks awaiting them on the conveyor belt. Anyway, the children being taught to tear apart books showed so much zeal that one little boy and one little girl sprained their little fingers struggling with the nasty covers of books that had rebelled, refused to capitulate, and while the children's teacher bandaged up their injuries, a few workers came to the rescue, spilling the insides of the recalcitrant books onto the conveyor belt with a flick of the wrist. The heavens may be far from humane, but I'd had about all I could take.

So I turned, went down the stairs, and was on my way out when I heard a voice call, "Hey, Haňt'a, you old loner, you! How does the new press grab you?" I turned back and saw a young man in a yellow baseball cap standing in the sun by the railing and holding up a bottle of milk in a theatrical gesture, like the Statue of Liberty. He was laughing and waving his bottle, they were all laughing, and I realized they knew who I was and even liked me, and all the time I'd been wandering around feeling crushed they'd been watching me and wondering if I was impressed with them and their gigantic new machine, and now they were laughing and waving their orange and baby-blue gloves in the air. I put my head in my hands and ran out of the room, away from their rich and varied laughter, down a long corridor lined with thousands of boxes of books, a whole run of books racing back as I lurched forward. I stopped at the end of it, unable to resist tearing open one of the boxes,

and what I saw was that the book the children had been
tearing apart, the book that took revenge on the fingers
of the little boy and little girl, was a prewar, preteen
adventure novel, and I pulled out one of the books and
looked on the last page, and there I learned that eighty-
five thousand copies had been printed, and since it was
in three volumes, over a quarter of a million books would
soon do vain battle with children's fingers. And as I
walked down other corridors, thousands of silent, de-
fenseless books passed before me like the chickens that
had broken out of their cages at the slaughterhouse in
Libuš, the chickens that waddled and pecked for a while
but were always caught by the girls, who then hung them
on the conveyor belt's hooks, thus condemning them,
like these books stacked along the corridors, to an early
grave.

If I could go to Greece, I said to myself, I'd make
a pilgrimage to Stagira, the birthplace of Aristotle, I'd
run around the track at Olympia, run in my underwear,
in long johns with shoelaces tied round the ankles, in
honor of all Olympic champions, if I could go to Greece.
If I could go to Greece with that Brigade of Socialist
Labor, I'd lecture to them on more than just philosophy
and architecture, I'd lecture to them on all the suicides,
on Demosthenes, on Plato, on Socrates, if I could go to
Greece with the Brigade of Socialist Labor. But they
belonged to a new era, a new world, it would all go right
over their heads, everything was too different nowadays.
Thinking these thoughts, I walked down the back steps
to my cellar and its murk and must, and began patting

the old drum's shiny, warped wood, when all at once I heard a scream, a mournful roar, and turned to find my boss glaring at me with bloodshot eyes, bellowing his rage over how long I'd been away and how both my cellar and his courtyard were clogged with wastepaper again, and although I didn't quite grasp everything he said, I felt how vile I was and how fed up with me he was, because he kept calling me a name no one had ever called me before—nitwit, nitwit, nitwit. First the gigantic press, then the Brigade of Socialist Labor and its summer tour of Greece, and finally me, in my world of moral contradictions, little me, the nitwit. So I worked the whole afternoon without a break, forked wastepaper into the drum as if it were the conveyor belt at Bubny, and much as the shiny book bindings flirted with me, I fought them off, repeating to myself, "No, no. You mustn't peek at a single book. Be as cold as a Korean hangman." I worked as though shoveling a pile of lifeless matter, and the machine worked with me, spluttering and twitching, its motor overheating, because it wasn't used to the tempo and had always been congested and rheumatic because of the cellar air. When I felt thirsty, I ran out and ran back across the courtyard with a bottle of milk, and even though each swallow was like a swallow of barbed wire, I didn't give up, I drank it a gulp at a time, the way I took cod-liver oil as a kid. Anyway, the milk was so awful that in two hours I'd cleared away enough paper to open up the hole in the ceiling again, which was important because it was Thursday, and every Thursday I waited with heart in mouth for the head of the Comenius Library to make his visit, and sure enough he came and stood over the opening with his usual basket of philosophy rejects, but when he emptied it, I didn't pick up the books that had fallen at my feet, I shoveled them straight into the drum, and even though I couldn't help noticing—my heart broke when I saw it—the *Metaphysics of Morals*, in it went with the rubbish, and on and on I worked, making bale after bale, no Old Masters this time around, a bale is a bale is a bale, I did only what I was paid for, my artistic days were over, and I realized that if I did only what I was supposed to do, I could be a one-man Brigade of Socialist Labor, and if I increased my output by fifty percent I could have a chance at the factory chalet in the mountains and, more important, a holiday in fabulous Greece—in other words, a chance to put on my long johns and run around the track at Olympia and pay my respects to Aristotle in Stagira. So I kept slurping milk and working, working inhumanly, unfeelingly, the way they worked at the gigantic press in Bubny, and in the evening, when I had finished and proved I wasn't such a nitwit after all, my boss, who was having a shower in the facilities behind the office, yelled out to me from under the spray that he wasn't going to waste any more time on me and had sent a letter to the higher-ups telling them to do with me as they saw fit.

I sat there for a while, listening to the boss drying himself off with his terry towel, and all of a sudden I felt a wave of nostalgia for Manča, who had written to me several times inviting me to nearby Klánovice, where she now lived, so I pulled a pair of socks over my dirty feet and ran out to catch the bus, and even though it was nearly dark by the time the bus let me off, I found someone who told me her address, and soon I was standing before a cottage in the woods with the sun going down behind it. But when I opened the door, I found nobody in the hall or the kitchen or any of the other rooms, so I went out into the back garden, and there I had even more of a shock than in Bubny. For there, against a backdrop of spreading pine and amber sky, stood a huge statue of an angel, as large as the Čech monument in Prague, and against the statue stood a ladder, and on the ladder stood an old man in a light-blue smock, white ducks, and white bucks, fashioning a beautiful woman's head out of the stone with his hammer, or rather fashioning a head that was neither male nor female, the androgynous face of a member of the heavenly host, and I saw him look down now and then at a woman sitting in a chair and sniffing a rose, I watched him transfer her features to stone with a chisel and a few light taps of the hammer, and that woman was my Manča. Manča had gray hair now, but she wore it in a kind of reformatory cut, a crew cut, like an athlete with a touch of spirituality; one of her eyes was lower than the other, which gave her a distinguished look, and if she seemed to squint a little, it was not because she had bad vision but because one of her eyes had simply got stuck while staring beyond the threshold of the infinite into the very center of an equilateral triangle, into the very heart of being, or, as a Catholic existentialist once put it, her defective eye symbolized the diamond's eternal blemish. Anyway, I stood there thunderstruck, and what struck me most of all was the statue's two big white wings, which looked like two giant white cupboards, and seemed to be in motion, feathers and all, as if Manča were flapping them lightly before soaring or after landing, and I could see with my own eyes that Manča, who had always hated books, who had never in her life read a book through except to lull herself to sleep, was ending her earthly days as a saint.

Meanwhile, twilight had given way to night, and while the old artist stood balanced on the ladder as if suspended from the sky, Manča gave me her hand and told me that the old man was her last lover, the last link in the chain of men she had known, and that since he could now love her only in spirit he had decided to compensate by building her a monument she could enjoy in the garden as long as she lived and place on her grave as a kind of coffinweight when she died. And while he worked on, perfecting the expression on the angel's face by the light of the rising moon, Manča showed me around the cottage, from basement to attic, explaining in hushed tones how an angel had come to her and she had obeyed him and taken up with a ditchdigger and spent all her savings on a plot in the woods, and the ditchdigger dug the foundation and slept in a tent with her, but then she threw him over for a bricklayer, and the bricklayer made love to her in the tent and put up all the walls, and then Manča took up with a carpenter and he did all the carpentry work and shared her bed, but then she threw him over for a plumber, who slept in the same bed as the carpenter but did all the plumbing, only to be replaced by a roofer, who both made love to her and laid her roof with concrete tile but was eventually replaced by a mason, who roughcast all her walls and ceilings by day and slept in her bed by night, until she took up with a cabinetmaker, who made all new furniture in return for her bed, and so it was that Manča, with nothing but a bed and a clear-cut goal, built herself a house. And now she had taken up with an artist, whose love, though platonic, was such that he had undertaken a statue of her in the form of an angel, which brought us back to where we began and completed the circle of Manča's life just in time to see the white bucks and ducks—the light-blue smock, having blended with the moonlight, was invisible—descend the ladder as if from heaven, and when his shoes touched ground, the hoary old man gave me his hand and said that Manča had told him all about me, that Manča was his muse, that Manča had rendered him so productive that he was now ready to continue the Almighty's work and make her an angel.

I returned to Prague on the last train, went home, and stretched out drunk and fully dressed under my two-ton canopy of books, and as I lay there thinking, I realized that Manča had unwittingly become what she never dreamed of becoming, that she had gone farther than anyone I'd ever known. I, who had constantly read books in search of a sign, never received a word from the heavens, while she, who had always hated books, became what she was meant to be, the kind of person people write about, and, more important, she had reached her full height. As I left, her wings shone in the night like two brightly lit windows in an Empire château; they had taken her far beyond our love story, beyond its ribbons and the turd she had brought back on her skis and promenaded in front of the Hotel Renner in the foothills of Golden Peak.

SEVEN

For thirty-five years I'd compacted wastepaper in my hydraulic press, never dreaming it could be done any differently, but two days after I laid eyes on the gigantic press in Bubny, the dreams I never dreamed came true. That morning when I got to work, who should I find in the courtyard but two of the Socialist Labor youngsters in their orange gloves, nipple-high blue overalls, suspenders, green turtlenecks, and yellow baseball caps, as if on the way to a game. My boss took them triumphantly down to my cellar and showed them my press, and in no time flat they had covered my table with a sheet of clean paper for their milk and made themselves at home, while I just stood there humiliated, stressed and strained, knowing all at once, knowing body and soul, that I'd never be able to adapt; I was in the same position as the monks who, when they learned that Copernicus had discovered a new set of cosmic laws and that the earth was no longer the center of the universe, committed mass suicide, unable to imagine a universe different from the one they had lived in and by up to then. My boss told me to go and sweep the courtyard or help out in the cellar or just stand there and do nothing, because next week I'd be making bales of clean paper in the cellar of the Melantrich Printing Works, clean paper, nothing else. Suddenly everything went black: I, who had spent thirty-five years compacting rejects, wastepaper, I, who couldn't live without the prospect of rescuing a beautiful book from the odious waste, I would be compacting immaculate, inhumanly clean paper! When I heard that, I was stunned, unstrung, I collapsed like a jumping jack on the first step of the cellar stairs, my arms dangling between my knees and a cracked smile on my face as I looked up at the two youngsters. They were not to blame, after all, they were only doing what they had been told; it was their daily bread, their job. I watched them pitching the wastepaper into the drum and pushing the red and green buttons, and I hoped against hope that my machine would go on strike or report sick or make believe its cogwheels or gearwheels were stuck, but no, on it churned at top speed, as if in the prime of youth, dinging and donging to beat the band, mocking me, showing me that only in the hands of Socialist Labor had it realized its true potential. And I had to admit that within an hour or two those youngsters might have been working in the cellar for years: they had divided up the labor between them, one of them scrambling to the top of the heap to provide a flow of paper and the other tending the drum below, so that in an hour they had made five bales. And every once in a while my boss would lean over the opening in the ceiling, give them a theatrical round of applause with his pudgy little hands, look over at me out of the corner of his eye, and shout down at them, "Bravo, bravissimo!" then add the Russian *"Molodtsy!"* and I would lower my eyes, wanting to leave but unable to make my legs move, I was so numb from the shame of it all and from the repulsive ding-dong of my machine announcing that the compaction would soon reach maximum. Just then I saw a book flying from the sparkling pitchfork into the drum, and I stood up, pulled it out, and, wiping it on my smock, held it to my chest for a while—as a mother presses her child to her breast, as Jan Hus in the statue in Kolín presses his Bible to his breast until it is half crushed by his body—and, cold as it was, the book warmed me. Anyway, I looked over at the boys and they looked back at me as if nothing had happened, so I summoned all my strength and glanced at the title, and yes, it was a fine book, Charles Lindbergh's account of the first transoceanic flight. And as usual I thought of Frantík Šturm, the sacristan of Holy Trinity, who collected books and magazines on the subject of aviation, because he was convinced that Icarus was Jesus' forerunner, the only difference being that Icarus fell from the sky into the sea, whereas Jesus was launched by an Atlas rocket, which can lift five thousand and eight hundred pounds to a three-hundred-and-fifty-mile orbit, and is circling

His earthly kingdom to this day. So I said to myself I'd make one last trip to Frantík Šturm's microbiotic laboratory with the story of how Lindbergh had crossed the ocean, and after that, farewell to small joys!

Tottering across the courtyard, I came upon my boss beaming: he was weighing a salesgirl by the name of Hedvička—first with the package of wastepaper she'd brought in, then by herself. He'd never change: what I felt for old books, he felt for young girls, and he never failed to weigh them—first with their paper, then without. He kept a little notebook of their weights and frolicked with them even when there were outsiders present, lifting them by the waist and placing them just so on the scale, as if planning to take their picture, and each time they came, he gave them a long lecture on the workings of the Berkel scale, constantly brushing against their arms and breasts, and whenever he showed how the dial worked, he stood behind them, as he now stood behind Hedvička—his hands on her hips, his nose in her hair inhaling rapturously, his chin pointing at the dial—and then back he jumped with a whoop, congratulating her on not having gained any weight, and after jotting down the result, he helped her off with a "Down you go," his arm around her waist again, and added, as usual, that now it was her turn to weigh him, and while she did, he whinnied at the top of his voice, trumpeted with glee like an old buck at the sight of a doe, after which Hedvička wrote out his weight on the frame of a door that went nowhere.

By then I was out of the courtyard, out in the sun,

but all I could see was gloom, and when I went into the church, I saw Frantík Šturm steel-wooling the altar as if it were a locomotive, his mind clearly elsewhere. He'd had his share of bad breaks, too: he used to love writing local items for the papers about broken legs, his specialty being Monday-morning reports of free-for-alls and riots that had ended in delirium and the nearest hospital or clink, and all he wanted was to go on writing about them for *The Czech Word* and *Evening News*, but then his father, who was a sacristan, died, and Frantík had to take over, and take over he did, but he didn't stop composing drunken brawls in his head. What's more, every time he had a minute, he would run off to his room in the presbytery, sink into the bishop's old armchair, and read everything he could get his hands on about new airplanes and their builders. And even though he had over two hundred airplane books, I could tell by the way he rubbed his hands and smiled when I gave him the book I'd found in my cellar, that it wasn't in his microbiotic library, and, watching his eyes fill with tears, feeling his gaze embrace me, I sensed once more that the days of my cellar's small joys were over: never again would I take Frantík Šturm a treat. And as we stood there, sheltered by the wings of two lame angels hanging from chains over the altar, a door opened noiselessly and the priest tiptoed in and told Frantík dryly to go and put on his robes: they had some last rites to administer.

So out I went into the sunny afternoon, stopping at Saint Thaddeus's prie-dieu and standing before him for a while, recalling how I used to pray to him to intercede for me on high and make those awful trucks that deliver the slaughterhouse paper sink in the Vltava, and how I used to enjoy pasting stars on my hat and kneeling there so I could hear the once-wealthy exclaim as they passed, "A good sign, the working classes crawling back to the Cross!" And as I stood there, my hat down over my eyes, I suddenly thought, Why not kneel and give it one more chance, why not pray to Thaddeus for a miracle? Because only a miracle would give me back my press, my cellar, and the books I couldn't live without. And just as I was about to go down on my knees, who should run into me but the philosophy professor, lost as usual, his glasses sparkling in the sun like two ashtrays. And since I was wearing my hat, he asked me, "How's the young man?" And I thought for a moment and said he wasn't in. "Heavens," said the professor, looking frightened, "I hope nothing's wrong." "No," I said, "he's just under the weather. But let me tell you straight out: there'll be no more Rutte articles, no more Engelmüller reviews." Then I took off my hat, and the professor looked even more frightened and, falling to his knees, he pointed up at me and cried, "You mean you're the young man and the old man, too?" I put on my hat again, pulled it down over my eyes, and said bitterly, "That's right. And no more *National Politics*, no more *National News*, you hear? I've been kicked out of the cellar." And when I started back to the building where I had worked for thirty-five years, the professor tagged along, bouncing up and down beside me, running in front of me, and pulling me by the sleeve. When he slipped me a ten-crown note and then added a five to it, I looked down at the money and said bitterly, "To help me look?" And the professor grabbed hold of my shoulder and, peering up at me through the thick lenses with his horsey eyes, he mumbled, "Yes, to help you look." "Fine," I said, "But for what?" "For better luck," he whispered, walking backward for a while and then turning and scurrying away as from the scene of an accident. And when I turned in to the entrance and heard the bell on my hydraulic press ringing away as gaily as if it belonged on a sleigh with a tipsy wedding party, I had to stop, I couldn't look at it, I retraced my steps to the street.

There I stood, blinded by the sun, not knowing where to go, and not a single phrase from the books I swore by came to my aid in this hour of need. So I shuffled back to Saint Thaddeus, collapsed on the prie-dieu, put my head in my hands, and slept or fantasized or phantasmagorized or maybe went slightly out of my mind with the injustice of it all, because as I knelt there, my hands against my eyes, I saw my press turn into the giant of all gigantic presses, a press so big, its four walls engulfed the entire city of Prague, and I saw myself pushing the green button, saw the press grinding into motion like a hydroelectric dam, and buildings tumbled like the mice in my old drum, like toys. I saw the walls advance, devastating everything in their path, and from my bird's-eye view I saw life in the center of town going on as usual though the outskirts were being devoured by the press's enormous jaws, and as all four walls zeroed in simultaneously on the main part of town, I saw stadiums and churches and public buildings on broad avenues and narrow side streets collapse, nothing could escape my Press of the Apocalypse. I saw the Castle cave in, and the dome of the National Museum, and the Vltava rose—the press was so powerful that the city might just as well have been wastepaper in my cellar—the walls picked up speed as they gathered together what they had demolished, and I saw myself as the Holy Trinity toppled over on my head, no longer seeing, but feeling myself being compacted and thrown together with bricks and timber and the prie-dieu, and then I could only hear, hear the trams and buses cracking as the walls came closer and closer, but there was still space among the debris, still air above the rubble, until the walls closed in and the air hissed and spouted its way up and out, churning together with the last human wails, and I looked up and saw an enormous bale standing on a deserted plain, a cube fifteen hundred feet long, maybe more, with all Prague compacted in it, myself included, all my thoughts, all the books I'd ever read, all my life, and it was all nothing more than the tiniest of mice being crushed with the wastepaper in my cellar by the Brigade of Socialist Labor.

When I opened my eyes, I was amazed to find myself kneeling on the Saint Thaddeus prie-dieu, and for a while I stared dumbly at a crack in the wood. But then I stood up and watched the cars going by, the red stripes left by passing trams, the people streaming along—people never stop in Spálená Street, they're all rushing from National Avenue to Charles Square or vice versa—and as I stood there, leaning against the presbytery wall to keep from being knocked over, out through the gates stepped Frantík Šturm, and after descending the stairs with great pomp, he turned as usual in the direction of our courtyard, caught sight of me, and as usual came up and bowed, inquiring, "Would you be Mr. Haňťa?" And pretending to be back in the courtyard, I replied as usual, "That is my name, sir," whereupon Frantík Šturm handed me an envelope, bowed, and retired to his room in the presbytery to change, because, as usual when I found him a book he could use in his library, he had put on his frock coat, stiff collar, and cabbage-leaf tie to add a touch of ritual to the letter he presented me with. And when I tore open the envelope, I found, as usual, a note on Frantík Šturm Microbiotic Laboratory stationery reading, "Dear Sir, In the name of the Frantík Šturm Microbiotic Laboratory we thank you for Charles Lindbergh's *The Spirit of St. Louis*, which will greatly enhance our collection. We trust you will continue to honour us with your favour. Yours sincerely, Frantík Šturm, Frantík Šturm Microbiotic Laboratory" and bearing a circular stamp that said "Frantík Šturm Microbiotic Laboratory" in the lower right-hand corner.

Deep in thought, I walked to Charles Square, where I tore up the thank-you note, knowing it was the last, because the days of small joys, small pleasures had come to an end: my press had tolled their knell, it had betrayed me. And as I stood in Charles Square looking up at the glimmering statue of Ignatius of Loyola cemented to the façade of his own church and outlined in trumpet-triumphant gold by his own halo, what I saw was a large gilt upright bathtub with Seneca lying upright in it just after he had slashed the veins in his wrist, thereby proving to himself how right he was to have written that little book I so loved, *On Tranquillity of Mind.*

EIGHT

Leaning against the counter at the open window in the cafeteria of the Black Brewery and drinking the local brew, I said to myself, "From here on in, my boy, you're on your own. You're going to have to force yourself to go out and see people and enjoy yourself, playacting until you give up the ghost, because from here on in it's just one melancholy circle after another and going forward means coming back, that's right, *progressus ad originem* equals *regressus ad futurum* and your brain is nothing but a hydraulic press of compacted thought." So there I sat in the sun, drinking my beer and watching the flow of people through Charles Square, youngsters all of them, students, and each had a small star on his forehead, a sign that each young person bears the germ of genius in him, and the eyes of each sparkled with vitality, the same vitality I used to have until my boss called me a nitwit. Leaning on the railing, I enjoyed watching the trams go back and forth, enjoyed their red stripes. I had all the time in the world now. I could go to the Franciscan Hospital and have a look at the first-floor stairs, which, or so the story goes, were made out of boards from the scaffold the Franciscans bought in 1621, after the flower of the Czech nobility was hanged from it in Old Town Square, or I could go to the Kinský Gardens, to the famous pavilion where, when you step on a button in the floor, a wall slides open and a wax figure comes out, much like the Petersburg chamber of horrors, where on a moonlit night a six-fingered freak stepped on the button by mistake and out came a wax-work tsar shaking a finger at him, as Yury Tynyanov described so well in "The Wax Figure." But I probably won't go anywhere, because all I need to do is close my eyes and everything I see is clearer than reality, and I prefer just looking at the passersby with their periwinkle faces.

When I was young, I had the same grand ideas about myself as they have, and for a while I thought all I needed, to be handsome, was a pair of sandals—the open kind, made of only a strap and a sole—and a pair of purple socks to go with them, so I bought the sandals and my mother knitted me the socks and I made a date for a Tuesday at the Lower Tavern: after all, the lineup might just have been posted early. So there I stood in front of the notice board examining the metal fitting around the keyhole until I felt ready to move in for the lineup, and even though the lineup turned out to be from the previous week, I read it through again, because I'd felt my right purple sock and sandal sink into something large and wet, and I didn't have the courage to look down. Anyway, I read it through again, all the way to the end, where my name was, and when I finally did look down, I saw that my sandal, the open kind with only a strap and a sole, had sunk into a large dog turd, so I tried reading the lineup through yet again, slowly, name by name, all eleven names on the second team, and then my name as substitute, but when I looked down, I was still standing in that awful dog turd. And when I looked up, who should I see coming out of her gate but the girl I had the date with, so I undid the strap, pulled my foot out of the purple sock, and left sandal, sock, and bouquet under the notice board of our soccer club and fled into the fields, where I sat and meditated on that fateful omen, because even then I had vowed to spend my life compacting wastepaper for the access it would give me to fine books.

Meanwhile I'd drunk several more glasses of beer and brought another back to the open window, where I was leaning against the counter, squinting into the sun, and thinking about whether I ought to go and have a look at the church at Klárov with its red marble statue of the Archangel Gabriel and that magnificent confessional the priest had had made out of boards from the box the Archangel Gabriel arrived in from Italy, but instead I closed my eyes blissfully and went nowhere, because as I drank my beer, I saw myself twenty years after the purple sock disaster walking through the outskirts of Stětín, where I chanced upon the local flea market, and at the tail end of the most down-and-out merchants I saw a man trying to sell a sandal and purple sock for the right foot. I could have sworn they were the ones, even the size seemed right, nine and a half, and I stood there dumbfounded at that man's faith, faith that a right-legged uniped in search of sandal and purple sock would happen by, that somewhere there was a cripple, size nine and a half, determined to make the journey to Stětín to buy a sock-and-sandal combination guaranteed to make him handsome. Beyond that man of great faith stood only an old woman selling two bay leaves, which she held up between two fingers. I left with a feeling of amazement: my sandal had come full circle—it had traveled around the world to stand in my way once more, a living reproach.

After returning my empty glass, I crossed the tram tracks and walked on, the sand in the park crunching underfoot like frozen snow, the sparrows and finches chirping. I looked at the babies in prams and the mothers on benches in the sun, their faces turned toward its healing rays; I stood before the oval pool, where naked children were playing, and noticed the stripes across their midriffs from the elastic in their pants. Hasidic Jews in Galicia used to wear belts of loud, vivid stripes to cut the body in two, to separate the more acceptable part, which included the heart, lungs, liver, and head, from the part with the intestines and sexual organs, which was barely tolerated. Catholic priests raised the line of demarcation, making the clerical collar a visible sign of the primacy of the head, where God in Person dips His fingers. As I watched the children playing naked and saw the stripes across their midriffs, I thought of nuns, who sliced head from face with one cruel stripe, stuffing it into the armor of the starched coif like Formula One drivers. Those naked children splashing away in the water didn't know a thing about sex, yet their sexual organs, as Lao-tze taught me, were serenely perfect. And when I considered the stripes of the priests and nuns and Hasidic Jews, I thought of the human body as an hourglass—what is down is up and what is up is down— a pair of locked triangles, Solomon's seal, the symmetry between the book of his youth, the Song of Songs, and the *vanitas vanitatum* of his maturity in the Book of Ecclesiastes. Suddenly my eyes were drawn to Saint Ignatius of Loyola and his glimmering trumpet-gold halo, and I thought how odd it was that while the statues of our great literary lights—Jungmann, Šafařík, Palacký— always sit stiffly in chairs and even the Romantic Mácha needs to lean against a column, our Catholic statues are full of motion, like athletes who have just spiked a ball over the net or finished the hundred-meter dash or a whirlwind discus throw, their sandstone eyes and arms raised as if on the point of returning God's lob or rejoicing in His victory goal.

I crossed the street and left the sun for Čížek's, which was so dark that the customers' faces shone like masks and their bodies were swallowed up by shadows, and as I walked down the steps into the restaurant, I read the following inscription over someone's shoulder:

Here stood the house in which Karel Hynek Mácha wrote his *May*. I took a seat, but quickly panicked when I looked up at the ceiling and saw the bulbs: it was just like my cellar. So I jumped up and ran out, and who should I bump into in front of the restaurant but an old friend who was drunk as a lord but immediately pulled out his wallet and, after riffling endlessly through some papers, produced a document from a detoxification clinic, which read: "This is to certify that the under-signed had no alcohol whatever in his bloodstream this morning." I folded it up and handed it back to him, and my friend told me how he had been planning to start a new life and had drunk nothing but milk for the past two days, and the milk had made him so woozy that his boss had sent him home that morning for drunken be-havior and docked him of two days off, but he went straight to the detoxification clinic, and when they'd done their tests and found that he hadn't a drop of alcohol in his blood, they picked up the phone and gave his boss what for, accused him of undermining the morale of a worker, so to celebrate his boss's rap on the knuckles and his own official bill of clean blood, he had been boozing it up and invited me to join him in what we used to call the Grand Slalom and which we had successfully completed, after many tries, one time only. It was so long ago I had forgotten most of the course, so my friend, whose name I had also forgotten, launched into an im-passioned description of it to win me over: we'd start off at the Vlachovka and move on to the Little Horn, then down to Paradise Lost and then to Myler's and the Coat of Arms, and at each place we'd order only one large beer, because we had to have time to make it to Jarolímek's and Láďa's and round the bend to the Charles IV and, after a detour down to the World Cafeteria, we'd go over to Hausmann's and the Brewery, and then across the tracks to the Good King Wenceslas and on to Pudil's or Krofta's, and finally Douda's or the Mercury before coming into the home stretch at the Palmovka or Scholler's Cafeteria, and if it wasn't too late, we'd cross the finish line at either Horký's or the Town of Rokycany. Running through the course, he clung to me drunkenly, but I finally shook him off and left Čížek's, crossing the luxuriant periwinkle patches of Charles Square, where the sun worshipers had moved from benches that were now in the shade to benches that were now in the setting sun. On my way back to the Black Brewery I had a glass of rum and then a beer and then another rum. Not until we're totally crushed do we show what we are made of.

Through the branches I watched the New Town Tower clock shining neon in the dark. As a boy I had dreamed of becoming a millionaire and buying phosphorescent hands and dials for all the city clocks. The mangled books made a final attempt to burst their bonds. Portrait of the artist as an old mushroom face. A breeze from the Vltava wafts through the square, I like that, I used to like walking along Letná in the evening, the river scent meeting the park scent, but now the river scent fills the street and I go into Bubeníček's, sit down, and order a beer absentmindedly, two tons of books perched over my head, a daily sword of Damocles I've hung above myself. I'm a schoolboy taking home a bad report card. The bubbles rise like will-o'-the-wisps. Three youngsters in a corner are playing a guitar and singing quietly, everything that lives must have its enemy, the melancholy of a world eternally under self-rejuvenation, that beautiful Hellenic model and goal, classical *gymnasia* and humanist universities. But in the sewers of Prague two armies of rats are locked in a life-and-death struggle. The right leg was a little frayed at the knee. Turquoise-blue and velvet-violet skirts. Helpless hands like clipped wings. An enormous side of beef hanging from the hook of a provincial butcher's. I hear toilets flushing.

Suddenly the door opened and in stomped a giant reeking of the river, and before anyone knew what was happening, he had grabbed a chair, smashed it in two, and chased the terrified customers into a corner. The three youngsters pressed against the wall like periwinkles in the rain, but at the very last moment, when the man had picked up half a chair in each hand and seemed ready for the kill, he burst into song, and after conducting himself in "Gray Dove, Where Have You Been?" he flung aside the halves of the chair, paid the waiter for the damage, and, turning to the still-shaking customers, said, "Gentlemen, I am the hangman's assistant," whereupon he left, pensive and miserable. Perhaps he was the one who, last year at the Holešovice slaughterhouse, put a knife to my neck, shoved me into a corner, took out a slip of paper, and read me a poem celebrating the beauties of the countryside at Říčany, then apologized, saying he hadn't found any other way of getting people to listen to his verse.

Having paid for my beer and three rums, I went out into the breeze and made my way back to Charles Square, where the brightly lit New Town Tower clock told a useless time: I had nowhere to go, I was floating in space. Then I found myself walking down Lazarská and turning into a side street, unlocking a back door, feeling along the wall for the switch, and when I turned on the light, there I was, back in my cellar, where for thirty-five years I'd compacted wastepaper in a hydraulic press. Why does Lao-tze say that to be born is to exit and to die is to enter? Two things fill my mind with ever new and increasing wonder—the starry firmament above me and the work I do, which is so terrifying it requires a divinity degree. Lining the drum with armfuls of wastepaper, I push the green button, the mice's eyes tell me more than the starry firmament, my tiny Gypsy girl comes to me half-asleep, and while the press grinds on like a helicon in the hands of a harmonica player, I remove the Hieronymus Bosch cover from my holy-picture-lined book box and find the book where the queen of Prussia, Sophie Charlotte, says to her chambermaid, "Do not weep. To satisfy your curiosity, I shall go and see what Leibniz himself was unable to teach me, I shall cross the boundary of being and nothingness." The bell rings, the red light comes on, the wall retreats, I put the book aside and fill the drum. Her body is covered with grease, she is as glib as ice when it begins to thaw. The gigantic Bubny press will do away with ten of the kind I use.

Messrs. Sartre and Camus have put it so well, especially the latter. The shiny covers flirt with me, and there is an old man in a blue smock and white shoes standing on the ladder. The dust swirls up with a brisk flap of the wings. Lindbergh flew over the ocean. I make myself a little bed in the wastepaper, I still have my pride, I have nothing to be ashamed of, like Seneca stepping into his bath I throw one leg over, then wait a bit and bring the other one over with a thud, then I roll up into a ball, just to see what it's like, and then I get up on my knees, push the green button, and roll back into the bed among the wastepaper and books, holding my Novalis tightly, my finger marking the sentence that has always filled me with rapture. I smile blissfully, because I am more and more like Manča and her angel, I am entering a world where I have never been and holding a book open to the page that says, "Every beloved object is the center of a garden of paradise." Instead of compacting clean paper in the Melantrich cellar I will follow Seneca, I will follow Socrates, and here, in my press, in my cellar, choose my own fall, which is ascension, and even as the walls press my legs up to my chin and beyond, I refuse to be driven from my Paradise, I am in my cellar and no one can turn me out, no one can dismiss me. A corner of the book is lodged under a rib, I groan, fated to leave the ultimate truth on a rack of my own making, folded in upon myself like a child's pocket knife, and at the moment of truth I see my tiny Gypsy girl, whose name I never knew, we are flying the kite through the autumn sky. She holds the cord, I look up, the kite has taken the shape of my sad face, and the Gypsy girl sends me a message from the ground, I see it making its way up the cord, I can almost reach it now, I stretch out my hand, I read the large, childlike letters: ILONKA. Yes, that was her name.